"The Last Thing I Want To Do Is Hurt You,"

Peyton whispered, nuzzling Tallie's ear with his nose. "I can't live your kind of life, you can't live my kind of life. You're not the type of woman who'd settle for an affair."

"How do you know what type of woman I am?"

"You're the type of woman who deserves more than I could ever offer." He allowed her to turn into his arms, knowing that if he didn't put a stop to their actions soon, there would be no turning back. He ached with wanting her.

"You haven't offered me anything. Yet."

Reaching deep within himself for his reserve willpower, Peyton shoved her gently away from him. "And I'm not going to offer you anything. Tonight I'm leaving, and I'm not looking back."

Dear Reader,

Welcome once again to Silhouette Desire! Enter into a world of powerful love and sensuous romance, a world where your most passionate fantasies come true.

September begins with a sexy, sassy MAN OF THE MONTH, *Family Feud* by Barbara Boswell, a writer you've clearly indicated is one of your favorites.

And just as exciting—if you loved Joan Johnston's fantastic HAWK'S WAY series, then don't miss CHILDREN OF HAWK'S WAY, beginning with *The Unforgiving Bride*.

The month is completed with stories from Lass Small, Karen Leabo, Beverly Barton and Carla Cassidy. *Next* month, look for a MAN OF THE MONTH by Annette Broadrick *and* the continuation of Joan Hohl's BIG, BAD WOLFE series.

So, relax, read, enjoy...and fall in love all over again with Silhouette Desire.

Sincerely yours,

Lucia Macro
Senior Editor

Please address questions and book requests to:
Silhouette Reader Service
U.S.: 3010 Walden Ave., P.O. Box 1325, Buffalo, NY 14269
Canadian: P.O. Box 609, Fort Erie, Ont. L2A 5X3

BEVERLY
BARTON
NOTHING BUT TROUBLE

SILHOUETTE *Desire*®
Published by Silhouette Books
America's Publisher of Contemporary Romance

SILHOUETTE BOOKS

ISBN 0-373-05881-0

NOTHING BUT TROUBLE

Books by Beverly Barton

Silhouette Desire

Yankee Lover #580
Lucky in Love #628
Out of Danger #662
Sugar Hill #687
Talk of the Town #711
The Wanderer #766
Cameron #796
The Mother of My Child #831
Nothing But Trouble #881

Silhouette Intimate Moments

This Side of Heaven #453
Paladin's Woman #515
Lover and Deceiver #557

BEVERLY BARTON

has been in love with romance since her grandfather gave her an illustrated book of *Beauty and the Beast*. An avid reader since childhood, she began writing at the age of nine and wrote short stories, poetry, plays and novels throughout high school and college. After marriage to her own "hero" and the births of her daughter and son, she chose to be a full-time home-maker, a.k.a. wife, mother, friend and volunteer.

Some years ago, she began substitute teaching and returned to writing as a hobby. In 1987, she joined the Romance Writers of America and soon afterward helped found the Heart of Dixie chapter in Alabama. Her hobby became an obsession as she devoted more and more time to improving her skills as a writer. Now, her lifelong dream of being published has come true.

To my dear friend, Jan Celeste Hamilton Powell,
whose ability to truly rejoice with me as well
as cry with me keeps our long-standing
relationship strong.

And a special thanks to Nancy Sue Elkins
and Brenda Hall, friends I can always count on
when I need them most.

Prologue

Tallulah Bishop swung open the door of her one-ton Chevy tow truck, ordered her Great Dane, Solomon, to *stay*, and grabbed her shotgun off the seat. Jumping down to the ground, she called out a warning to the drunken man a few yards away.

"Cliff Nolan, you let Richie go right now, you hear?"

Holding his young son by the nape of his neck, Cliff turned his head sharply, sneering at Tallie. "Get the hell off my property, you damned nosy do-gooder. This here's my land and my family. I'll do whatever I damn well please."

Richie's small mongrel dog growled at Cliff, who immediately thrust out his big foot and kicked the animal.

"No, Daddy, don't. Please don't hurt Whitey," Richie cried when he heard his dog yelp in pain.

Tightening his hold on Richie, Cliff swung the boy around several times and tossed him to the ground. Richie reached out for Whitey, circling the dog's neck with his thin little arms and looking up with tearful, pleading eyes at his staggering father.

"Hell's toenails," Tallie muttered to herself, then she shouted out again to Cliff. "Leave Richie and Whitey alone or I'll shoot you. Do you hear me?"

Cliff Nolan stared at Tallie, his bloodshot hazel eyes half-closed, his thin lips curved into a smirk. "You ain't nothing but hot air. Always coming around here, putting ideas in my Loretta's head. She don't need the likes of you telling her how to be a wife. You wouldn't know the first thing about being a woman."

"I know that no man has the right to beat his wife and kids or mistreat his animals." Tallie took several tentative steps away from the gravel driveway and into the weed-infested yard.

Loretta Nolan crept out onto the porch of her mobile home, her haggard face appearing far older than her twenty-seven years. "Please, Cliff—"

"Shut your trap, woman!" Cliff glared at his wife.

"Best you go, Tallie," Loretta said.

With his arms wrapped around Whitey's neck, Richie Nolan crawled away from his father, dragging his dog with him. Shifting his feet in the dust, Cliff turned halfway around, stared down at the escaping twosome and raised his leg.

"No, Daddy, don't!" Richie shouted just as Cliff's foot came down on the dog, who yelped in pain.

Lifting his foot again, Cliff kicked at Richie, but missed his target when the boy scooted away. Still holding a trembling, whimpering Whitey, Richie kept pushing himself farther and farther away from his rampaging father.

"This is my last warning, Cliff. Get away from Richie. Now!" Tallie aimed her shotgun.

Cliff Nolan raised his foot. Richie froze in horror when he bumped into the side of the house. Drawing back his leg, Cliff aimed his foot for a kick into Richie's stomach. Tal-

lie screamed. Cliff turned sharply in her direction. With
Whitey in his arms, Richie stood up quickly and ran toward the front porch. Unsteady on his feet, Cliff spun
around and bellowed for Richie to stop.

"Leave him alone," Tallie warned.

"Go to hell!" Cliff said.

Tallulah Bishop pulled the trigger on her shotgun.
Birdshot ripped through Cliff's ragged jeans, splattering
across his back, butt and legs. Yelling in pain, Cliff
dropped to the ground.

Still clinging to Whitey, Richie flung himself and his dog
into his mother's open arms. Loretta stood on the porch
steps, her dark-circled eyes staring at her husband in disbelief.

"Call the sheriff," Tallie said. "And an ambulance, too.
Cliff's going to need Doc Hall to pick that birdshot out of
his butt."

Nodding in silence, Loretta turned slowly and walked
back inside her mobile home. Richie stood on the porch,
holding Whitey close to his little chest while tears streamed
down his dirt-streaked face.

Tallie supposed she should go over and see if she could
help Cliff, who lay on the ground in a heap, his skinny behind sticking straight up in the air while he moaned and
groaned and cursed everything from heaven to hell. But
Tallie wasn't inclined to offer either sympathy or assistance. The ambulance would be here soon enough, and it
was unlikely that Cliff would bleed to death from birdshot
splattered into him from yards away.

The sheriff probably wouldn't be far behind the ambulance. Even though Lowell Redman didn't like Cliff any
better than she did, he'd have no choice but to arrest her.
After all, she had shot a man.

Now she'd have to call Peyton. He'd be madder than a
wet hen. He'd warned her the last time she'd had to call him
for help that he was tired of bailing her out of one jam af-

ter another. But what should she have done, just stood there and allowed Cliff to abuse Richie and Whitey? For over a year, she'd been begging Loretta to take the kids and leave, but her pleas had fallen on deaf ears.

Tallie knew she'd done something really stupid this time, and whether she wanted to or not, she'd have to ask Peyton to come get her out of jail. And if there was a trial, she'd need him to defend her.

She dreaded facing Peyton far more than she dreaded spending the night in jail. No matter how good her intentions were, she always wound up creating problems for him, and she really didn't want to cause him any difficulties, especially not now when he was thinking about running for governor. Peyton Rand was a good man and deserved only the best—and the best for him certainly wasn't Tallie Bishop.

As bad as she hated to admit it, maybe Peyton had been right when he'd told her that she was nothing but trouble.

One

Tallie could tell by the look on his face that he was spitting mad. There was a ruddy hue to his tanned skin, a cold fire in his deep blue eyes and a coiled tension in the way he moved. His salon-styled ash blond hair appeared slightly mussed, as if the wind had dared to tousle it. Glancing at Deputy Wanda Simple, Tallie smiled, straightened her shoulders and prepared herself to endure his wrath. Although Peyton Rand was usually a calm, controlled, easygoing man, Tallie knew she possessed the power to dent his Southern-gentleman facade.

He slammed his leather briefcase down onto the table. Leaning over slightly, he splayed his big hands on each side of the briefcase, then glared at Tallie.

"You've done some stupid things before, Tallulah Bankhead Bishop, but this has to be the—"

Oh, he was really angry. He'd called her Tallulah! "I warned him to stop, Peyton. I promise I did." Tallie took several steps forward, her hands cuffed behind her back.

"He was beating Richie. Kicking him around. I couldn't just stand there and let him hurt that child, now, could I?"

Straightening to his full six-foot-two height, Peyton bent his arms at the elbows and threw open his hands, knotting his palms into half-closed fists. "Okay, so you had to do something to stop him, but did you have to shoot Nolan with birdshot?"

"What was I supposed to do?" Tallie inched her way toward Peyton, one cautious step at a time, looking up at him with what she hoped was a remorseful expression on her face.

"You had Solomon with you, didn't you?" Peyton reached out and grabbed Tallie by the shoulders, giving her a gentle shake. A shiver of awareness zipped through his body, reminding him of why he shouldn't touch Tallie. Regardless of his unwanted attraction to the woman, the fact remained that she was bad news. "Why didn't you let Solomon handle Cliff Nolan?"

"Hell's toenails, Peyt, if I'd let Solomon attack Cliff, I'd be in here on murder charges instead of assault."

"You're going to be able to get her off, aren't you, Mr. Rand?" Wanda Simple asked. "This whole town knows Cliff Nolan is a no-good skunk, always manhandling Loretta and those kids. Tallie just did what she thought was right."

"Well, I hope the judge will see it that way." Releasing his hold on her, Peyton shook his head. Why, dear God, why had he been cursed with the responsibility of Tallie Bishop? If ever there were two people on earth who were a mismatched set, it was Tallie and him. "I came straight from Jackson, so I haven't had a chance to talk to Clayburn about your bail. But I have talked to Lowell, and you can thank him that the charges aren't assault with intent."

"I've already thanked him." Tallie realized that nothing she said or did would soften Peyton's attitude, and she couldn't much blame him. Ever since her brothers had left

Crooked Oak to find their own way in the world, Peyton had acted as their substitute, trying to look out for his friends' kid sister—a kid sister who, at twenty-six, should have known better than to shoot a man.

"I'll see if Clayburn won't go ahead and set bail so I can get you out of here today." Peyton glanced at Tallie's arms, arched behind her back to accommodate the handcuffs. "Wanda, take this little heathen to her cell until I can make arrangements with Judge Proctor." Pointing his index finger at Tallie, he said, "It would serve you right if I left you in here all night."

Thrusting out her chin, Tallie gave him a haughty stare. "You do whatever you want to do, Peyton Rand. I splattered Cliff Nolan with birdshot to keep him from doing any more harm to his child and the child's dog. I hate that I had to shoot him, and maybe what I did was wrong, but if you can't see past the law into the human heart, then I doubt—"

"Dammit, woman, will you shut up!"

With a startled jerk, Tallie tensed, then swallowed hard and glanced up into Peyton's stern face. "You tell Judge Proctor that if I could have thought of another way to handle the situation, I wouldn't have filled Cliff with birdshot, but... at the time, I saw no other alternative."

"I'll tell him, and maybe he'll agree to set bail."

"Do you have any idea how much bail will be?" Tallie didn't have a lot of cash money, but her garage and tow-trucking business was quite successful, so she didn't think there'd be a problem with posting her own bail.

"I'll handle the bail," Peyton said. "I can trust you not to leave the country, can't I?" A hint of a smile twitched at the corners of his mouth.

And Lord, how Tallie loved his mouth. She'd spent endless hours wondering just what it would feel like to kiss that mouth.

Taking a deep breath, Tallie didn't even try to disguise the sense of relief she felt knowing that Peyton's anger had begun to subside. She grinned at him. "I won't even leave the state."

"That's good to know." Retrieving his briefcase, Peyton headed for the door, all the while chiding himself for being a total fool. No matter how many times her behavior created problems for him, he could never stay angry with Tallie. Despite her fierce independence and feminist bravado, she was a tenderhearted, vulnerable woman—somewhere beneath all that grease, the boyish haircut and her aggravating take-charge attitude.

"Oh, Peyt, would you please go by the Humane Shelter and pick up Solomon?" Tallie asked. "I had Wanda call Susan to come get him and keep him until we could straighten out this mess."

"We'll pick up Solomon after you're released." Peyton stopped just inside the doorway, turned around and surveyed Tallie from head to foot. "How the hell can such a little woman stir up so many stinks in this county and cause me nothing but trouble?"

Before Tallie could reply, Peyton left. She supposed she should be grateful that he'd even bothered to come when she'd called. After all, he really didn't owe her anything. Just because Peyt's father, old Senator Rand, had been a hunting and fishing pal of her grandfather's and just because her brothers and Peyton had buddied around together—despite the differences in their social positions—didn't mean he was responsible for getting her out of every mess she got herself into, did it? Of course not. But ever since Jake and Hank and Caleb had, one by one, left Crooked Oak for the big, wide world outside the boundaries of Tennessee, Peyton had become her guardian angel, always just a phone call away. Of course, he fussed and fumed and swore she'd be the death of him. And whenever she called him for help, he warned her, "This is the last time, so help me, Tallie."

"Come on, Tallie, let's get you into a cell until Mr. Rand comes back for you." Wanda Simple, a tall, skinny, bespectacled woman in her early thirties had graduated from high school with Jake, and she and Tallie had been on friendly terms for years.

"Do you think Clayburn Proctor will go ahead and set bail so I can get out of here today?" Tallie asked.

"Ah, shoot, Tallie, you know Judge Proctor thinks the world of you. Why, ever since you saved his grandson's life when you got to the scene of the wreck before the ambulance and performed CPR on that child, Judge Proctor's thought you hung the moon." Placing her hand on the small of Tallie's back, Wanda led her down the hall toward the short row of jail cells. "Besides, Peyton Rand could charm the birds down from the trees, couldn't he?"

Tallie stood perfectly still, while Wanda uncuffed her. "Yeah, you're right. Peyton's got his daddy's silver tongue. He's a born politician."

"I swear, girl, why haven't you made a move on that man? It's plain to see that you're crazy about him, and everybody in the county knows he's always acting like your knight in shining armor."

"Peyt just feels responsible for me, that's all." Tallie walked into the cell. "My brothers made him promise to keep an eye on me."

Wanda closed the cell door. "Well, for a man who doesn't care, I'd say he keeps a pretty close eye."

"He's never thought of me as anything but a pest. Besides, I'm hardly the kind of woman a man like Peyton Rand would want, and I'm certainly not what he needs." Stepping away from the bars and into the center of the small cell, Tallie spread out her arms and slowly turned around in a circle. "Just look at me. I'm a country girl. What I need is a man with calluses on his hands and dirt on his boots, not some rich lawyer who wants to be governor."

"You look fine." Wanda ran her gaze from the top of Tallie's head to the tips of her feet. "Well, you could use a little dolling up, but that wouldn't be too difficult with your face and figure. And even if you and Peyton Rand are totally different, that doesn't mean you weren't meant for each other. Opposites attract, you know?"

"Wanda, a man on the verge of running for governor isn't about to get himself romantically involved with a woman who owns a tow-trucking company, has only a junior college education and is always getting into trouble because she can't keep her nose out of everybody else's business."

"Well, if you don't make a move soon, you're liable to lose him for good," Wanda said. "He's been dating that Donna Fields for three months now. You know her granddaddy was governor and her uncle's a federal judge."

"Peyton and I are all wrong for each other, but he and Donna Fields are a different matter. She'd probably make him the perfect wife." Tallie hated admitting that another woman was far more suitable for Peyt than she was, but the truth was the truth. Donna Fields was the best possible choice for a politician's wife. Tallie Bishop would be a politician's nightmare.

Peyton sat in the luxury of his dark blue Jaguar, his shoulders resting comfortably against the leather seat as he spoke on his cellular phone. With casual grace, he flicked the ashes off the end of his cigar into the tray.

"She's never gotten herself into this much trouble before, Clayburn, but she honestly thought she was doing the right thing."

"I know," Clayburn Proctor said. "Tallie's got a good heart, it's just that she acts without thinking. I don't have a problem with setting her bail now. No sense in that girl

staying overnight in jail. But there's no way we can get out
of a trial. Of course, since Lowell's only charging her with
assault and battery, I can just put the case on my docket if
she pleads guilty. No need to take this before a jury."
Clayburn laughed. "But my bet is if it did go to a jury,
they'd acquit her. I know she broke the law, but by God,
somebody's needed to do something about Cliff Nolan for
a long time. If only his wife would press charges against
him."

"Thanks, Clayburn. I appreciate this." Peyton hadn't
had a doubt that the judge would bend over backward to
help Tallie; as a matter of fact, there was hardly a soul in
the whole county, especially around Crooked Oak, who
wouldn't go out of their way for Tallie Bishop. Just about
everybody liked her. Despite her penchant for getting into
trouble, Tallie's main fault was that she was always trying
to help others. He'd never known anyone so concerned
about every living creature on earth. He supposed that was
the main reason he'd never been able to sever the ties that
bound him to Tallie, despite the many times he'd wished
she'd get the hell out of his life.

"Well, who's going to post bond for Tallie?" Clayburn
asked.

"I am." Peyton laughed. "She's promised me that she
won't leave the country."

"Well, since you're the one posting bail, I'd say that a
fair amount would be $1,678. Wouldn't you say that would
be fair?"

Hearing the slight chuckle in Clayburn Proctor's voice,
Peyton took a draw on his cigar, then blew out a ring of
smoke. Damn the man! The judge had a warped sense of
humor. Whoever heard of such an odd amount for bail?

"That's a rather unusual sum, don't you think?" Peyton asked.

"You know, for some reason that amount sticks in my
mind. I seem to connect $1,678 with you, Peyton."

"It couldn't possibly be the exact amount you've lost to me in our friendly little poker games over the last few months, could it?

"Well, well, that must be the reason."

"Clayburn, you're not going to get that money out of me. Tallie won't jump bail."

"Not intentionally," the judge said, chuckling loudly. "But knowing Tallie, she just might take that tow truck of hers into Mississippi without even thinking, and if she does, and if I have a mind to, I can rule that she's jumped bail."

Clayburn Proctor was a wily old fox who enjoyed his games. Peyton wouldn't put anything past him. If anyone else had been posting Tallie's bail, Clayburn would have named a different amount, but the judge couldn't resist the chance to needle Peyton. "You wouldn't do that to Tallie."

"Probably not," Clayburn admitted. "We're both under that girl's spell, aren't we, Peyt? Like everybody else in these parts."

"You may be under her spell, but I'm damn well not!" Peyton had never been under any woman's spell and most definitely not Tallie Bishop's. She was five-feet-two-inches of pure trouble. She'd been a pest as long as he'd known her, ever since she'd been a kid and traipsed around after him and her brothers when they went hunting and fishing. And, dammit all, when she'd turned sixteen and fancied herself in love with him, she'd nearly driven him crazy until he'd persuaded her that there could never be anything romantic between them.

"Don't protest so much," Clayburn said. "Folks will assume you've got something to hide."

"Thanks again for setting bail, odd amount or not," Peyton said, deliberately changing the subject. He was not interested in Tallie Bishop, most definitely not in the way Clayburn Proctor was suggesting. They were barely friends. He tried to look out for her as a favor to her brothers and because somebody had to do it. There was nothing more to their relationship than that—absolutely nothing.

Standing in the doorway, Peyton watched Tallie while she made the rounds up and down the pens in the animal shelter. When she and Susan Williams, the shelter manager, stopped by the pen that housed Solomon, the huge dog reared up against the wire gate, his head towering over the two women.

The moment Susan opened the gate, Solomon jumped down and loped out toward Tallie. Squatting beside the Great Dane, Tallie gave him a hug, then ran her hand down his back in a loving pet.

"Did you think you were doomed to life in this prison?" Tallie's voice held the same soft, even quality a mother uses when reassuring a child. "Well, Peyt and I have come to take you home, but you'll have to be on your best behavior because you'll be riding in Peyt's Jaguar."

Good God! He hadn't thought about that when he'd offered to drive Tallie and Solomon home. That dog was the size of a pony. Peyton felt like kicking himself. Why hadn't he let her call on someone else for taxi service? Why did he think it was his responsibility to make sure she got home safe and sound?

"Where's your truck?" Susan asked as they walked into the outer office area where a volunteer manned the reception desk.

"Mike picked it up at the Nolans' and took it back to the garage." When Tallie stopped, Solomon came to heel without a word from his mistress. "We didn't know whether or not I'd be spending the night in jail." Smiling, she cut her eyes in Peyton's direction. "Lowell let me bring Solomon along in the police car, and I certainly appreciate y'all taking care of him for me."

"Good gracious, Tallie, taking care of Solomon is the least we could do for our number-one volunteer," Susan said. "Mr. Rand, we're certainly glad you were able to get Tallie out of jail so fast. I just can't believe she'll have to stand trial for protecting a child and his dog."

"Well, Ms. Williams, Tallie did shoot a man." Peyton knew it was useless to point out Tallie's faults to any of her many admirers, and Susan Williams was no exception. "I expect once I present the evidence, Judge Proctor will go easy on her."

"As well he should," Susan said. "I just wish we could get Loretta to take those children and leave Cliff Nolan. If she doesn't, he'll wind up killing one of them sooner or later."

"Tallie, we really should be going." Peyton nodded toward the front door. "I've taken off all afternoon, but I need to get back to Jackson. I have a dinner engagement in Marshallton this evening."

"Sure thing." Tallie, her dog at her side, gave Susan a quick hug. "Thanks again. Come on, Solomon."

Just as Peyton opened the door and stepped outside, the telephone rang. When the volunteer informed Susan that the call was for her, Tallie followed Peyton outside. But before they made it to the car, Susan stuck her head out the door and called to Tallie.

"Wait up," Susan said. "Tallie, I need to talk to you for just a minute. It's important, or I wouldn't hold you up like this."

Tallie gave Peyton a questioning look. "Do you mind terribly? I promise I'll hurry."

"Two minutes." Peyton tapped the face of his Rolex.

"Stay, Solomon," Tallie ordered, then rushed to the entrance of the animal shelter where Susan stood waiting.

Peyton leaned against the side of his car, his tense body striving for relaxation. Reaching inside his coat pocket, he removed his sunglasses and put them on, then crossed his arms over his chest.

He didn't have time for this delay, whatever the cause. He'd had his secretary clear his calendar for the afternoon because he hadn't had any idea how long this latest "Tallie rescue" would take. But he and Donna had plans to dine with Marshallton's mayor tonight. Peyton wanted to get his old friend's thoughts on the possibility of running for governor in the next election.

Peyton glanced over at Tallie. The late-afternoon sun caught in her raven hair, giving it a blue-black luster. She kept her dark curly hair cropped short, in an almost boyish style, but there was nothing boyish about that baby-doll face, those long, thick eyelashes, that full pink mouth. Damn, why couldn't she have stayed skinny and flat-chested, the way she'd been at sixteen when she'd professed her undying love and he'd gently rejected her? Somewhere between the age of sixteen, when Caleb, the youngest of the Bishop boys, had left for college on a baseball scholarship and had asked Peyton to look out for his little sister, and the age of eighteen, Tallie Bishop had blossomed. Actually, she'd over-blossomed. Her body had filled out in all the right places, creating an hourglass-shaped body on a petite frame.

Peyton noticed the way her frayed blue jeans clung to her hips and legs. She wore a grease-stained short-sleeved chambray shirt, tucked beneath the waistband in the back and hanging loose in the front. Underneath the unbuttoned shirt, her full breasts strained against a faded yellow T-shirt. On a less well endowed woman, the clothes would have looked masculine. On Tallie, they looked damned sexy. And that was the problem. For the past eight years, men had been ogling Tallie, despite her tomboyish ways. She'd had her pick of most young bucks in the county, dating every good-looking Tom, Dick and Harry. On more than one occasion, she'd coldcocked some overzealous suitor. Trouble sought Tallie the way a moth seeks a flame.

And it wasn't just the men who couldn't take no for an answer that caused problems, it was Tallie's constant interference in other people's lives. He had to admit that she was a good citizen, working in her spare time as a volunteer fire fighter for Crooked Oak as well as a helper at the Humane Shelter. But more often than not, Tallie let her concern overshadow her better judgment. Case in point—filling Cliff Nolan full of birdshot. But there was always something. Her love for animals had gotten her into trouble with Lobo Smothers, an illiterate farmer suspected of illegal hunting and trapping. Tallie had been doing everything in her power to help the authorities catch him and put him in jail. Needless to say, she and Lobo weren't the best of friends. And there were her endless efforts to get abused women to leave their husbands and start new lives. Cliff Nolan wasn't the only husband in Crooked Oak who had a bone to pick with Tallie.

What the hell was Peyton going to do about her if he did decide to run for governor? There was no way the woman would ever change, and having his name linked with hers in connection to one of her wild exploits was bound to damage his image.

His image? His old man had always cared about the Rand family's image, and it had been one of the things he'd despised about his father. If he did decide to enter politics, would he become more and more like Senator Marshall Rand? His father had died a lonely and unhappy man. Peyton didn't want to follow in his footsteps.

"Ready?" Tallie asked.

Peyton stared at her, unaware until she'd spoken that she had approached the car. "All finished with Susan?"

"Ah...yeah...just some shelter business." Tallie opened the passenger door, ordered Solomon inside and slipped into the seat.

Peyton didn't like the way she'd answered him. She was hiding something. Tallie was so damned honest, the truth showed on her face whenever she tried to lie. Pink spots stained her cheeks. Getting into the Jag, he started the engine. "What sort of business?"

"Huh?"

"What's up, Tallie?" Peyton backed out of the parking area. "If this is something that's going to cause me any more problems, then let me hear it now."

"What makes you think this has anything to do with you?" Sticking out her chin, Tallie crossed her arms under her bosom.

"If it's not something that could get you into trouble, then why won't you tell me?" Turning the car onto the highway, Peyton glanced over at Tallie and wished he hadn't. Her slender, crisscrossed arms had boosted her full breasts up and out, reminding him of how truly female she was.

"An anonymous caller told Susan that he had information about where Lobo Smothers had set up some traps, out toward Kingsley Hill."

Peyton groaned, then glanced over at Tallie. "Stay out of it. Give the information to Lowell and let him handle it."

"I could do that, but it won't do any good. Lobo Smothers always seems to be one step ahead of the law."

"Lowell Redman is just newly elected. Give him a chance."

"The last time I shared information with the sheriff's department, they arrived at the scene to find no traps, and no Lobo. I told you then that Lowell's got a rat working for him. I just haven't figured out who it is yet, but I will."

"Tallie, stay away from Lobo Smothers." Peyton issued the command in a tight, controlled voice. "The man is dangerous."

"All the more reason that he should be behind bars! Besides, rumor has it that Lobo is growing marijuana out there in the woods somewhere. If his abuse of animals won't stir the law into action, maybe his being in the drug racket will.''

''Whatever Lobo Smothers is doing, let the law handle it! Dammit, woman, you're in enough trouble. In another week or two, you'll be going to trial for shooting a man full of birdshot. You do realize that if Lowell Redman wasn't a friend and if Clayburn Proctor didn't think you were a saint for saving his grandson's life, you could do some serious jail time for what you did.''

''I was defending a poor, helpless child and a pitiful little dog from a monstrous brute.'' Solomon growled as if agreeing with his mistress.

''Tallie, I've been getting you out of trouble for years now, and I'm sick and tired of it. I've tried to talk reason to you, but you refuse to listen.''

''There's no need for you to waste any more of your valuable time, Peyton,'' Tallie said, refusing to look in his direction. ''Just drop Solomon and me off at the garage.''

''Fine. I'm probably running late, as it is.''

''Well, that's just awful, isn't it? You sure wouldn't want to keep Donna Fields waiting.''

''No, I wouldn't want to keep Donna waiting. Ladies like Donna are accustomed to a certain kind of behavior from the men they date . . . like being punctual for dinner.''

''Ladies like Donna?'' Tallie turned in her seat, stretching the safety belt to its limit when she leaned toward Peyton. ''A lady whose grandfather was governor and whose uncle is a federal judge? A lady professor with blue blood in her veins? My, my, a lady like that could do a lot for a man with political aspirations. Just think what a wife she'd make for someone with his eye on the state capitol.''

Peyton glanced at Tallie and then back at the road. He knew she was trying to goad him into a fight. She was implying that his only interest in Donna was her suitability, and he didn't like to think he'd become so much like his father, he would consider marrying a woman just because she and her family could help him politically.

"Donna is a very special lady. I'll have to introduce you to her sometime." Peyton turned off the highway into the parking area for the garage and tow-truck company Tallie owned and operated with Mike Hanley and his sister, Sheila Vance.

"Spare me." The moment Peyton killed the engine, Tallie opened the door. "I doubt Donna Fields and I have anything in common. Someone with blood as blue as hers would probably be offended by a little ol' redneck like me."

Peyton laughed at the thought of introducing Donna and Tallie. The funny thing was, he had the oddest notion that once they met, the two women would actually like each other. "Don't count Donna short just because of who she is. She's not a snob."

Tallie got out of the Jag, then ordered Solomon to join her. "Well, you and Donna have a pleasant dinner tonight, and don't you worry about me. There's not one reason for you to bother with me again until my trial."

"I hope you're right," Peyton said. "I'll call you when Clayburn lets me know about the trial date."

"Fine." Leaving the door open, Tallie walked away, then stopped and turned around. "Thanks, Peyt. I... well, just thanks."

"Tallie?"

"Huh?" She walked back over to the Jag. "Let Lowell Redman handle Lobo Smothers."

"Yeah, sure."

"I mean it. You stay out of trouble."

"I'll try." She slammed the door.

Waiting until Tallie and Solomon disappeared inside the garage, Peyton pulled the Jag out onto the highway and headed toward Jackson. Something told him that he'd be seeing Tallie again before the trial. If she stayed out of trouble for two weeks, it would be a minor miracle.

Two

Peyton placed the stadium seats on the metal bleachers and assisted Donna into her place at his right while his brother Spence sat down on his left. Since his brother had married Pattie Cornell and become the instant father of two teenagers, Peyton had taken his role as an uncle quite seriously. J.J., Spence's stepson, was a varsity player on Marshallton High's baseball team, and Peyton tried to make as many Saturday-night games as possible, but this was the first time he'd asked Donna to accompany him.

Over the last ten years since Peyton had devoted himself to building a successful private practice, he'd given up more and more of his leisure time and had forfeited a personal life altogether. He'd dated a lot, but had never become seriously involved. Between work and his duties as Tallie's guardian angel, he hadn't found a woman willing to accept the limited time he had to offer a relationship.

Several months ago, he'd met Donna at a political fundraiser. They had liked each other immediately, and when he'd asked her out, she'd accepted. She didn't seem to mind that he was dedicated to his career. She taught history at a local college and was devoted to her students. Although half the state of Tennessee already had them engaged, they considered themselves good friends, neither of them in a hurry to commit to anything more.

"I hope you aren't doing this just to be a good sport," Peyton said to Donna. "I know coming to a high school baseball game is hardly the ideal date."

"Don't be silly." Donna smiled, her cinnamon-brown eyes sparkling with warmth. "I really like your brother and his family. And this is a real treat. I've never been to a baseball game."

"Sweetbriar Seminary for Young Ladies didn't have a baseball team?"

"We had a volleyball team, but I didn't play and seldom went to the games. I lived with my nose stuck in a book. And in college, I was too busy keeping up my grades to waste time on anything except the football games Uncle James took me to when he visited his alma mater."

Peyton laughed, trying to imagine Donna as a college girl. At thirty, she was such a serious-minded woman that he had a difficult time thinking of her any other way.

Spence punched Peyton in the ribs. "You two ready to get something from the concession stand? It's our treat since we invited y'all to the game."

Pattie Rand leaned over her husband to touch Peyton's arm. "Why don't you and Spence take our orders and go for the food while Donna and I get better acquainted."

Although Peyton knew Pattie would give Donna the third degree while he and Spence were at the concession stand, he reluctantly agreed. The lines at the stand were long. Undoubtedly most baseball fans had decided to dine at the field tonight. The aroma of hamburgers and potatoes frying mixed with the milder smell of hot dogs and cotton candy, while the mouth-watering scent of roasted peanuts wafted through the early-evening air.

Peyton glanced around at the multitude of ball fields that comprised this section of the park, then past the enormous parking area to the lighted tennis courts, the outdoor Olympic-sized pool and the newly constructed recreation center.

"This is quite some place, isn't it? There was nothing around here like this when we were kids playing ball." Spence put his hand on his brother's shoulder. "We did good, don't you think, donating most of the old man's money to build this place."

"Yeah." Peyton knew how difficult it had been for Spence to agree to christening this modern recreational facility the Marshall Rand Memorial Park. Spence had hated the old man, and hadn't gotten along with Peyt for years because he'd once thought him a carbon copy of their father.

"Are you still considering running for governor?" Spence asked.

"You think it would be a mistake, don't you?" Peyton stepped forward a couple of inches when the snail-paced line finally moved.

"I think you'd run the risk of following in the old man's footsteps." Spence glanced down at the order list his wife had given him.

"I wouldn't be the kind of politician the Senator was." Peyton glanced around, checking to see if anyone seemed interested in their private conversation. Lowering his voice, he said, "I'd like to make a difference for the people of this state. There are so many things that need to be done, and I truly think I could accomplish a great deal."

"You're a smart man, Peyt, and I think a fairly honest man—" Spence grinned "—for a lawyer."

"Hey there, little brother, I resent that slur."

"Politics can change a man. He can start worrying more about his image than he does about the people who elected him in the first place. Marshall Rand never did anything that wasn't for the good of Marshall Rand." Spence followed Peyton a few steps closer to the concession stand as the line progressed slowly. "You're a better man than Father was, but you're a lot like him. You look like him, talk like him... you definitely inherited his way with words. Hell, man, you even picked up his bad habit of smoking cigars."

"I've cut back. I'm down to a handful a day, usually one after lunch and one after dinner, so don't start on me about my cigars. Tallie gives me enough grief over my smoking. I don't need any scolding from you."

"Now there's a woman who could keep a politician in line," Spence said. "Hey, any word on when she'll go to trial for shooting Cliff Nolan?"

"That shooting only occurred three days ago, and it seems to be the talk of the county." Peyton wasn't surprised. News always traveled fast in small towns and rural communities where everybody knew everybody and neighbors tended to keep tabs on one another. "Clayburn cleared some time on his docket for next week. He's bending over backward to be fair to Tallie and still stay within the law."

"Tallie told us all about what happened. Pattie and I ran into her here at the ball field the night after she got out of jail." Spence looked from side to side, taking note of the people in line and the crowds out in the adjoining fields where the bleachers were filled with cheering observers. "She's probably here tonight. She comes with Sheila Vance to all of Sheila's little boy's games."

Peyton groaned. "That's all I need! I can't see a minute's peace for that woman."

"I don't feel a bit sorry for you. When she gets into trouble and calls you for help, all you have to do is refuse."

"You know I promised her brothers I'd keep an eye on her. They were well aware of what a little heathen she is. I swear, Spence, I never knew a woman could cause a man so much grief. I thought things would improve when she got older, but I think they're getting worse."

"I guess you know there are plenty of men who'd like to be in your shoes," Spence said.

"What the hell are you talking about?"

"I'm talking about the fact that, underneath those blue jeans and grease, there's quite a woman. Smart, caring, sensitive and pretty. You seem to be one of the few men around these parts who hasn't realized there's a sexy woman hiding behind that grease-monkey facade of Tallie's. Now, I wonder why that is?"

Peyton didn't want to answer his brother's question. To find the answer would involve some deep soul-searching where his relationship with Tallie was concerned, and that wasn't something he intended doing. He had too many mixed emotions when it came to that damned irritating female. A part of him wished that she'd simply disappear off the face of the earth. Then another part of him couldn't imagine his life without her—without thinking about her, worrying about her, taking care of her... wanting her.

The customer ahead of Peyton and Spence paid for his food, leaving them first in line at the concession stand window. Spence placed their order, then waved at someone two lines over. Peyton's glance followed his brother's. The bottom dropped out of his stomach. Tallie Bishop, her hands filled with a tray of food and drinks, walked toward them, a warm smile of greeting on her face. Solomon stood at her side, and accompanying them was Mike Hanley, her muscle-bound business partner.

"Hi, there." Tallie rushed over to Peyton, Solomon following her. "You here to watch J.J.'s game?"

"Yes, Donna and I came with Spence and Pattie." Peyton wasn't sure why he wanted Tallie to know that Donna was with him. Maybe it was because of the way Mike stood so close to her, as if he was proclaiming ownership.

"Well, Danny's game will be over soon. I just might drop by and watch the rest of the varsity game." When Peyton made no comment, she turned to Spence. "Eric Miller is here, and he's been drinking. I thought about calling Lowell and seeing if he'd send over a deputy, but he'd just tell me he couldn't arrest Eric unless he caused a problem."

"I wish that man would stay home when he's drinking. He's such an embarrassment to Tony." Pulling his wallet from the back pocket of his jeans, Spence took out several bills to pay for his order and laid the money down on the counter. "If he gives you any trouble, Tallie, let me know."

"I can handle Miller if he starts bothering Tallie." Mike draped a protective arm around her shoulders.

"Who is Eric Miller and what's this all about?" Never taking his eyes off Tallie, Peyton reached out and picked up one of the cardboard food trays.

"Eric's son Tony plays varsity ball with J.J. Half the time, Eric shows up at the games three sheets to the wind," Tallie said. "He harasses the umpire, curses the players and creates problems for his son. At the first game of the season, Miller caused such a ruckus, he wound up spending the night in jail."

"Yeah, and even after he found out that Tallie was the one who called the sheriff, he wouldn't leave her alone," Mike said.

"What do you mean he wouldn't leave her alone?" Peyton asked.

"Well, it seems Miller has the hots for our Tallie. He's been giving her a rough time lately," Spence said. "The guy doesn't want to take no for an answer."

"Why didn't you tell me about Miller?" Peyton glared at Tallie.

"There was no reason to bother you." Tallie tightened her hold on her food tray. "Solomon acts as a deterrent.

Believe me, even Eric Miller doesn't want to take him on. Besides, at that first game when he got really obnoxious, I called Lowell and he took care of things."

"Couldn't you avoid the man?" Peyton asked. "You could stay away from these games. You're not a parent."

"Neither are you! Besides, I'm not going to let the likes of Eric Miller keep me from doing whatever I want to do and going wherever I want to go."

"Well, that first game when you called Lowell, you could have stayed out of it and allowed the other fathers to handle everything, including calling the sheriff."

"They were too busy trying to drag Eric off the field," Tallie said defiantly. "They sort of had their hands full since the man is six foot two and weighs close to two-fifty."

Peyton took a deep breath, releasing it on a loud sigh. "This food is going to be cold if we don't get it back to Donna and Pattie," he told Spence, wondering why he ever bothered trying to talk sense to Tallie. She always had a rational explanation for everything she did, regardless of the consequences.

"Yeah, you're right." Spence turned to Tallie. "I'll keep an eye out for Miller. Come on on over when the Little League game ends. We'll introduce you to Peyt's lady friend."

"I'll do that." Thrusting out her chin and sticking her nose in the air, Tallie gave Peyton a see-if-I-care-who-you're-with smile.

Peyton grumbled under his breath as he and Spence made their way back to the field where the game had just begun.

"What's the matter, big brother?" Spence asked. "Don't you think it's time for the two women in your life to meet?"

"The two women in my... Tallie Bishop is not a woman in my life. She's a pest. A nuisance. A thorn in my side. But she is definitely not a woman in my life."

"Sure. Whatever you say." Spence grinned from ear to ear.

Thirty-five minutes later, Tallie waited with Sheila Vance for her son's coach to finish the after-game pep talk and instructions on when the Little League team would practice next. A cool springtime night breeze reminded the women that summer was nearly two months away. Tallie zipped up her black and yellow jacket.

"Are you planning to go over to the varsity game to meet Donna Fields?" Sheila asked. "I think Mike was hoping you'd leave when we did."

"Ever since Mike's divorce, he's had some crazy notion that the two of us would make a great team. I've tried to tell him that being business partners and friends is all there is ever going to be between us." Tallie ran her fingers through her short, windblown hair, lifting her curly bangs off her forehead.

"Give him time and he'll get the picture." Sheila buttoned her beige cardigan sweater. "Even if Mike can't be the man, I wish someone would come along and wake you up to the fact that Peyton Rand is not the only man in the world."

"I know he's not the only man in the world. It's just that—well, he was the first man I fell in love with...and there hasn't been anybody else."

Releasing her indrawn breath on a loud huff, Sheila shook her head. "I don't understand you, Tallie. If you want Peyton, why don't you go after him? Use your feminine wiles on him."

"I didn't say I wanted him." Tallie kicked at the ground with the tip of her black tennis shoe. "Besides, I don't think I have any feminine wiles. Growing up with only a grandfather and three big brothers, I didn't learn much about being female."

"Pooh! You don't have to learn to be female. It's just something you are. And believe me, honey, you're all female. What you have to do is go over there and show Peyton Rand that you're more woman than that Donna Fields could ever be."

"How do you suggest I do that?"

"First, admit that you want Peyton Rand."

"I *don't* want him." When Sheila looked at her skeptically, Tallie shook her head. "I can't want him. He's all wrong for me, and I'm all wrong for him. You know as well as I do that if he runs for governor, he'll need a wife like Donna Fields. Someone sophisticated and educated. Someone with the right background."

"Don't sell yourself short," Sheila said.

"I'm not," Tallie said. "I know that I'm smart and hardworking and have more friends than a person has a right to, but I know my shortcomings just as well. Peyton and I just aren't right for each other."

Mike, who'd been waiting at the fence for Danny, walked the boy over to where Sheila and Tallie were talking. "Ready to go, ladies?"

"Tallie's staying to see the rest of the varsity game." Accepting the baseball glove her son handed her, Sheila put her arm around him. "I need to get Danny home for a bath and then bed so we won't be late for Sunday school tomorrow."

"Are you sure you want to stay?" Mike asked Tallie.

"I'm sure," Tallie said. "I've heard so much about Donna Fields that I think it's high time I met her."

Mike shrugged, then turned and walked away with Sheila and Danny, who both gave Tallie farewell waves.

Taking time to shore up her courage, Tallie waited a few minutes before strolling over to the field where the varsity game was being played. She spotted Peyton sitting next to an attractive redhead, who sported a rust leather coat almost the same color as her dark auburn hair.

Standing at a distance, Tallie glanced back and forth from the action on the field to Peyton. Peyton wasn't exactly sitting in the stadium seat; he lounged in a relaxed position, sort of sprawled out, half sitting, half lying. Feeling her heartbeat quicken, Tallie cursed her stupid weakness. The very sight of Peyton Rand excited her. Of all the men she knew, why did the most unsuitable one have to be the one who gave her butterflies in her stomach?

She and Peyton came from such diverse backgrounds. He from a wealthy, political aristocracy. She from a family of poor blue-collar rednecks. He was a brilliant, sophisticated lawyer; she was a country girl who drove a tow truck. He was a man who played by society's rules, and she had spent her entire life breaking all those rules, living by her own set of ethics.

So what if she and Peyton Rand were doomed as a couple? That didn't mean that Donna Fields was the right woman for him. It wouldn't hurt if she just went over and checked Donna out. After all, she couldn't call herself a true friend if she let just any woman come along and snag the man she'd always dreamed would someday be hers.

Readjusting the collar on her jacket, Tallie took a deep breath, inhaling and exhaling very slowly. Solomon crawled under the bleachers and lay down in the dirt when Tallie made her way upward, finding an empty spot directly below Peyton and Donna. She spoke to Spence and Pattie, exchanging pleasantries while she settled into place.

Tilting her head slightly, she leaned back toward Peyton. When he didn't respond, she sat up straight, glancing out across the field to the scoreboard. "I see Marshallton is behind by two points. What we need is for J.J. to hit another home run the way he did at last Saturday's game."

"I don't know if we could put up with him if he hits another homer," Pattie said. "For days, he had such a big head, we threatened to disown him."

"The boy has a right to be proud. He's a good player. One of Marshallton's best," Spence said.

"Spoken like a proud stepfather." Peyton wondered what it would feel like to have children, even stepchildren with whom you shared a close relationship. In the last few years, he'd given marriage and parenthood more than one passing thought. After all, he wasn't getting any younger, and it never hurt a politician to have a family.

Turning around in her seat, Tallie stared at Donna Fields. "Hi, I'm Tallie Bishop, an old friend of Spence's and Peyt's."

Donna's big brown eyes widened. "Ah, so you're Peyt's little Tallie."

Tallie wasn't certain what the other woman meant by her comment. Obviously, Ms. Fields knew more about Tallie than Tallie knew about her. "I'm not sure that I'm—"

"I've had to cancel more than one engagement with Donna because of you." Peyton slipped his arm around Donna's shoulders. "She's been an absolute sweetheart by being so understanding."

"How absolutely...sweet of her." Tallie glared at the auburn-haired beauty, who flashed her a brilliant smile, not a trace of animosity in her expression.

"You're somewhat like Peyton described you," Donna said. "But he forgot to tell me how pretty you were."

Now why had that woman gone and said something nice to her? Tallie wondered. She'd been bound and determined not to like Donna Fields, and here she was all friendly and nice and... Tallie wanted to hate her, but she knew right off that that was going to be impossible.

"Thanks for the compliment," Tallie said. "I'm afraid Peyt hasn't told me anything about you, but I've drawn my own conclusions. You're not quite what I was expecting."

"What exactly were you expecting?" Donna asked.

"Tallie..." Peyton narrowed his eyes, glowering at her, his expression filled with warning.

"Oh, calm yourself, Peyt. I'm not going to say anything to embarrass you. I like her." Tallie held out her hand to Donna. "It's very nice to meet you, Ms. Fields."

Donna accepted the friendly greeting, shaking hands with Tallie. "It's very nice to meet you, too, Tallie. And please call me Donna. I have a feeling you and I are going to be friends."

"Yeah, something tells me that we are." In that one moment, in a flash of brilliant female intuition, Tallie knew that Donna Fields wasn't in love with Peyton. Love wasn't there in her eyes when she looked at him, or her voice when she spoke to him, or in her touch when she placed her hand on his arm.

Peyton didn't like this new turn of events. His gut instincts had told him that, once they became acquainted, Tallie and Donna would like each other, but he hadn't counted on it happening so fast. Both women shared qualities that drew others to them, and he had to admit that Donna's friendliness, her concern for others and her warm, caring nature had reminded him of Tallie. But that was where the similarities ended. Donna would be an asset to any man; Tallie would drive a sober man to drink.

While the game continued, Tallie and Donna talked, discussing various subjects, but somehow their conversation kept reverting to Peyton Rand. The man himself appeared oblivious to everything the two women said about him. Pattie joined their conversation from time to time, but most of her concentration centered on her son, the team's pitcher.

In the bottom of the sixth inning, the score tied five to five, Tony Miller came to bat. When the umpire called his third strike on the boy, Eric Miller marched over to the fence and yelled out a condemning obscenity.

"Oh, good Lord, I wish that man would stay home," Pattie said.

Peyton took a good look at this Miller fellow. He was about the same height as Peyton, but outweighed him by at least thirty pounds, most of which were contained in his enormous beer belly. The very thought that this middle-aged, foulmouthed drunk had made sexual advances to Tallie made Peyton furious. If the man ever touched her...

Tallie stood, stretching her arms out on each side, allowing the feeling to return to her numb backside. "I've got to make a pit stop. Do either of you need to go?" She glanced at Donna and then at Pattie.

"Yes." Grinning at Tallie, Pattie stood. Donna shook her head no. Tallie and Pattie made their way down the bleachers to the ground. When Solomon saw Tallie, he crawled out from his resting place and followed the two women toward the recreation center.

"Wonder why she called me Peyton's 'little Tallie'?"

"What?" Pattie asked.

Tallie waved and spoke to several people they passed on the path to the rest room. "Wonder why Donna Fields referred to me as Peyton's 'little Tallie'?" she repeated.

"I think it just slipped out before she thought about what she was saying. Peyton didn't seem to approve, did he?"

"Peyton Rand would like nothing better than to see the last of me." Tallie pushed open the door marked Women, then held it for Pattie. "Stay, Solomon."

"Peyton talks about you all the time, you know." Pattie waited in line with Tallie.

"Yeah, I'll bet he does. He probably tells you what a holy terror I am and how he's always having to get me out of trouble."

"I think Spence and I know almost everything about Tallulah Bankhead Bishop. From the time you were a kid following your big brothers around, to your recent arrest for shooting a man with birdshot. You're Peyton's favorite subject, and the strange thing is, he's not even aware of it."

"Don't you get sick and tired of hearing about me?"

"The question is don't you think Donna Fields would be sick and tired of hearing about you after three months?"

"What makes you think he talks to her about me?" Tallie asked.

"I'd bet my last dime he does." Pattie smiled at Tallie. "If Donna thought she and Peyton had a future together, she'd have every right to be terribly jealous of you, and she isn't. Didn't you notice?"

Just as Tallie started to reply, two women emerged from the stalls, leaving them free for Tallie and Pattie. By the time they came back out and washed their hands, the bathroom had cleared and they were its only occupants.

"She's not in love with Peyt, is she?" Tallie dried her hands on brown paper towels.

"Donna told me that she thinks Peyton is a wonderful man and she enjoys his company." Punching the air dryer, Pattie rubbed her hands together. "But no, I don't think she's in love with him. She's a widow, you know, and I believe she has some unresolved feelings for her dead husband."

"Do you think Peyt's in love with her?"

"No."

"Then why... I mean... well..."

"Why have they become an item?" Smiling, Pattie sighed. "Peyton is thirty-six and considering running for governor, so it's only natural that he'd think about needing a wife. He hasn't realized yet that although he and Donna are good friends, they'd be terrible as lovers."

"Then Peyt and Donna aren't... I mean..."

"Donna Fields is not your competition, Tallie."

"What do you mean? If I've given you the impression that I'm interested in Peyton, in that way, then—"

"There's no need for you to lie to me," Pattie said, opening the rest-room door.

Following Pattie outside, Tallie signaled to Solomon. "I guess I've wanted Peyt since I was sixteen and realized I was in love with him. But I'm the worst woman in the world for him. He's told me himself that all I am to him is trouble."

"I'm not so sure about that." Pattie walked beside Tallie and Solomon as they made their way back toward the ball fields. "Considering what Peyton's told me about you, I admit that you might prove a liability to a politician. On the other hand, you're a champion of some very popular causes, and people seem to like you."

"I can't believe this conversation." Stopping abruptly, Tallie turned to the other woman. "I dreaded meeting Donna because I knew she'd be everything that I'm not, that she'd be perfect for Peyt and that I'd hate her because she'd be such a haughty, nose-in-the-air snob. But I like her, and now you're telling me that she isn't my competition, that she and Peyt aren't lovers, that—"

"I'm trying to convince you that you're the right woman for Peyton Rand?"

"Hush, Pattie, don't say that out loud."

"Why not?"

"Because it isn't true. After meeting Donna tonight, I know she really is perfect for a man like Peyt and I most definitely am not."

"There's only one problem. Peyton and Donna are not in love. She may be perfect for a man *like* Peyton, but not for Peyton."

"Peyt and I are like oil and water, you know." Tallie caught sight of Eric Miller's hulking frame moving toward her at a rather rapid pace for an overweight man who was weaving around like a toddler just learning to walk. "Oh, no," Tallie groaned.

"What's wrong?" Pattie asked just as Eric staggered up between them, his big body accidently shoving into Tallie, unbalancing her momentarily.

"Hey there, sexy gal. You interested in going out to my truck with me for a little drink?" Eric swayed toward Tallie, his breath reeking of alcohol.

"I think you've had one too many little drinks," Tallie told him.

Slipping his arm around Tallie's waist, Eric pulled her up against him. "I don't know why you keep saying no. It ain't like you've done got a man."

Struggling against his powerful hold, Tallie glared up at Eric. "Let me go, you damned fool. Don't you know Solomon would rip your throat out if I gave the order."

As if on cue, Solomon snarled, baring his sharp teeth. The hairs on his back bristled.

"I ain't scared of no damned dog. I could probably break his neck."

"Tallie, I'll go get Peyton and Spence," Pattie said, walking away hurriedly.

"No, don't," Tallie called, but Pattie didn't respond. "Eric Miller, you're a menace to society."

"You ain't gonna sic that dog of yours on me, and we both know it." Eric squeezed Tallie so fiercely, she cried out. "If you're gonna be mine, sexy gal, you'd better learn to like it rough."

Tallie counted to ten. He held her so tightly, she could barely breathe. If only she could manage to loosen his hold on her, she could aim her knee at his groin. He was right, she didn't want to sic Solomon on him, but if she couldn't free herself, she might have no other choice.

"Look, you overgrown baboon, if you don't let me go, I will sic Solomon on you!"

Eric lowered his face downward until his nose touched Tallie's. "Give me a little taste of what I want."

That was it. She'd had all she was going to take. Just as she opened her mouth to give Solomon an attack order, she felt Eric's hold on her loosen. Glancing behind Eric, she saw Peyton Rand, his big hand gripping Eric's shoulder.

"Let the lady go." Peyton's voice held a cold, deadly edge.

Eric lumbered around, glaring at Peyton as he jerked himself out of the other man's hold. "Who the hell are— Oh, yeah, you're that fancy-pants lawyer Tallie's so hung up on, ain't you?"

"I'm the man who's telling you that if you ever lay a hand on Tallie again, you might not live long enough to regret it."

Eric chuckled, the sound loud and filled with nervous bravado. "Are you threatening me?" Eric puffed out his chest, his big gut only inches away from Peyton's firm midsection.

"I'm stating a fact. Leave Tallie alone or, if I can't put you behind bars, I'll handle you personally."

"Yeah, you and what army?"

Tallie stood there staring at Peyton as if she'd never seen the man before in her life. What was he doing? Did he even realize the implication of what he was saying? It wouldn't look good if the papers picked up this story: Potential Gubernatorial Candidate Threatens Man's Life Over Woman.

"You didn't have to come running over here to protect me," Tallie said, planting her hands on her hips. "I was about to sic Solomon on him."

"Stay out of this, Tallie," Peyton told her.

"Stay out of this?" Tallie noticed Spence coming up behind his brother, followed by Pattie and Donna Fields.

"Need any help, Peyt?" Spence asked.

"I think I can handle this," Peyton said. "What do you think, Miller?"

"I think I ain't fool enough to take on two men." Eric turned, his heavy-lidded eyes resting on Tallie. "Next time, I'll wait for a more private spot to sweet-talk you."

When Peyton reached for Miller, Tallie ran between the two men. "Go on, Eric, get out of here!"

"Ain't that sweet. You're worried I'll bloody up pretty boy's face," Miller said.

"No, I'm afraid Peyt will knock your brains out and get arrested for murder." Tallie grabbed Peyton's clenched fist. "Let him go."

With a grin on his fleshy, blotched face, Miller walked off, swaying slightly as he made his way toward the parking lot.

Grabbing Tallie by the arm, Peyton pulled her down the walkway, away from the small crowd of onlookers, including Donna, Spence and Pattie. Following along peacefully, Solomon sniffed the air.

"What do you think you're doing?" Tallie jerked away from him just as they rounded the corner of the concession stand.

Peyton moved toward her, his gaze riveted to her face. He shoved her up against the back wall of the concession stand and splayed his hands out on each side of her head as he glared down at her. "What the hell am I supposed to do with you?" His voice shook. His hands trembled.

"That wasn't my fault," Tallie said. "Besides, I didn't ask for your help. It was Pattie's idea to tell you what was happening. Solomon and I had everything under control." She peered around Peyton to where her dog sat a few feet away, sniffing the trash cans. "Just as soon as the trial is over, I'll never ask for your help again."

"Is that right? Are you going to be able to stay out of trouble with three men in this county ready to do you bodily harm? Cliff Nolan wouldn't hesitate to beat the hell out of you, that goon Miller seems the type quite capable of rape and there's not a doubt that Lobo Smothers would kill you or anyone else who gets in his way."

"I've got a gun. I've got a dog. I'll take care of myself. It's not like anything is actually going to happen to me, you know."

"Are you stupid, woman? Dammit, you are. Nolan, Miller and Smothers are all dangerous men. You need a keeper. Your brothers knew that when they asked me to watch out for you."

"I do not need a keeper!"

Gripping her shoulders tightly, Peyton gave her a sound shake. Beads of perspiration dotted his forehead and upper lip. He wanted to break her in half. He wanted to shake her until her teeth rattled. He wanted to turn her over his knee and spank her until she promised to behave herself. But more than anything, he wanted to pull her into his arms and kiss the breath out of her. The very thought of anything happening to Tallie scared the hell out of him.

"Promise me that you won't go near Cliff Nolan's family or get yourself involved in any scheme to try to catch Lobo Smothers. And if Eric Miller comes near you again, call Lowell Redman immediately."

It took every ounce of willpower she possessed not to throw herself into Peyton's arms and ask him to hold her. She could sense the anger inside him, but she sensed something else, too. He was afraid for her, genuinely afraid.

"I will be on my best behavior from now until the trial. I promise." She couldn't bear to think she might be the cause of any negative publicity for Peyton. After all, the very fact that he was representing her at her trial would probably make the newspapers, at least locally. She didn't want to do anything else that might create problems for him if he did decide to run for governor.

Peyton eased his hold on her shoulders. He should release her immediately, but damn, he couldn't let her go. Not yet. Touching Tallie was a mistake. He knew better. Just the feel of her tense little shoulders beneath his big hands aroused him. His mind had told him over and over again how wrong he and Tallie were for each other. Unfortunately, his body had ideas of its own. But he couldn't allow his lust for her to overrule his common sense. She was ten years too young for him. Her brothers were his friends. He didn't dare let her know how he felt or she'd jump to all the wrong conclusions. No sir, he wasn't about to take advantage of Tallie when all he wanted from her was sexual release.

"Try to stay out of trouble, will you, for both our sakes?" Stepping away from Tallie, Peyton dropped his hands to his sides. His stomach tightened into knots when he looked at her. Those big, pale brown eyes, that full, pouty mouth, that stubborn little chin. Damn, why couldn't he feel this way when he looked at Donna?

"I never mean to cause trouble for you, Peyt."

"I know, Tallie. I know."

"I guess you'd better get back to your date and let Spence and Pattie watch the rest of the ball game," Tallie said.

"I suppose you're right." Turning around, Peyton hesitated before walking away from her.

"Oh, Peyt."

He glanced over his shoulder. "Yeah?"

"I like Donna. She's a very nice lady. She's just perfect for you."

"Yeah, you're right. She is perfect for me," Peyton said. She's everything I could want in a wife. There's only one problem. She doesn't turn me inside out the way you do, little heathen.

Tallie watched Peyton walk away, back to where Donna stood by the bleachers waiting for him. He was where he belonged—with a woman he could be proud of, a woman his intellectual and social equal, a woman who could help his political career, not rip it to shreds.

Three

———

Sprawled out in the fat, navy-blue leather chair, Peyton sat alone in his Jackson apartment, a glass of Scotch in one hand, a half-smoked cigar in the other. He'd taken Donna home forty-five minutes earlier, after making a total fool of himself by coming on to her. She'd gently but forcefully told him that they were not going to have sex. He supposed he should be grateful to her for having more sense about the matter than he did, but damned if he could, considering his state of arousal. It had been quite some time since he'd been with a woman. In the past, his casual relationships with women had afforded him protected and uncomplicated sex. Donna was a different matter. She'd told him in no uncertain terms that she wasn't about to play stand-in for another woman. When he'd told her there was no other woman, she'd laughed in his face.

Donna was a smart lady. Too damned smart. She'd figured out right away that his interest in Tallie Bishop was a lot more than big brother protector. Of course, he had denied that wanting Tallie and knowing he couldn't have her kept him in a state of sexual frustration most of the time.

During the past ten years, he'd been able to keep his desire for Tallie under control, first by telling himself she was just a kid, and then by making sure he always had a willing bed partner in his life. But things had changed in the last few years. Tallie wasn't a kid any longer, and his bed partners had, by his own choice, become few and far between.

The problem was that he wanted Tallie, but he didn't dare allow himself to love her. Although she'd make most any man a good wife, Peyton couldn't see Tallie as first lady of the state. She wasn't the kind of woman who'd make a good political partner. No, Tallulah Bankhead Bishop might be the sweetest, prettiest, most desirable woman he'd ever known, but she wasn't suited to the kind of life-style he'd chosen for himself.

And he was as ill suited to Tallie's life-style as she was to his. He could never be the kind of man she needed. He was far too set in his ways, far too entrenched in his family's traditions to break free. He was not the rebel his younger brother had always been. No, Peyton Marshall Rand played the game by the world's rules. He was an expert at unemotional combat. He knew what it took to win and was willing to pay the price. That's why he never lost.

Controlled by her emotions, Tallie Bishop lived by her heart's desires, always championing the underdog, always trying to right all of life's wrongs. Never considering the outcome, she jumped into situations with both feet.

If Tallie hadn't once fancied herself in love with him, he might have already thrown caution to the wind and bedded her. But he couldn't take the chance that she'd really fall in love with him and he'd wind up breaking her heart. Tallie deserved better than a brief affair—an affair he could use to work her out of his system.

Peyton lifted the snifter to his lips, sipping the aged Scotch, savoring the smoky flavor of the heady whiskey.

Images of Tallie filled his mind. Curly black hair tousled by the wind. Pale, milk-chocolate eyes staring at him with such unabashed longing. Soft, pink lips, moist and tempting, whispering his name. Small, sure hands caressing his body.

He swallowed the remainder of the Scotch in one large gulp, then coughed on the strangling strength of the liquor.

Damn! He had to stop thinking about Tallie. There had to be some way to get her out of his mind. If only Donna...no, that wouldn't work. And it wouldn't be fair to Donna or to himself.

Of all the women on earth, why did Tallie have to be the only one who could elicit such strong feelings in him? She made him angry, she made him laugh—she made him horny as hell. Every time he saw her, he wanted her. Every time he touched her, it was all he could do to stop himself from dragging her off to the nearest bed. Tallie brought out every possessive, protective instinct in him. And to make matters worse, he knew she wanted him just as much as he wanted her.

But, God in heaven, they would be disastrous for each other. They'd make each other miserable. Somewhere out there, the fates were laughing themselves silly. Peyton Rand and Tallie Bishop were totally wrong for each other. The only problem was that their bodies didn't realize the fact.

Tallie tossed and turned in her bed. She had a splitting headache that half a dozen aspirin couldn't cure. What had caused the problem? Stress? Tension? Worry about the upcoming trial? Peyton Rand?

Tallie threw back the cotton floral sheet onto the muted navy-blue and rust-red plaid coverlet folded at the foot of her antique metal bed. Moonlight streamed through the open windows. A cool, late-night breeze swayed the long floral curtains that matched the dust ruffle on the bed.

Solomon, who lay on a hand-hooked rug near the door, raised his head, looked at Tallie, then readjusted his relaxed position. Sheba, the mixed-breed cat Tallie had adopted from the Humane Shelter, slept curled atop the old leather-and-wood steamer trunk at the foot of the bed.

Picking up her yellow terry-cloth robe, Tallie slipped her arms through the sleeves and tied the belt. What she needed was something soothing to drink. Hot tea. No, hot chocolate. The chill of the May night and the cool wooden floor beneath her feet reminded Tallie that she hadn't put on her house shoes before she'd made her way across her bedroom and out into the hallway.

Tallie flipped on the light switch in her pristine white, but hopelessly cluttered kitchen. She glanced out the row of long, uncovered windows onto the moonbeam-kissed backyard, the trees and grass gilded with sheer gold, the black sky encrusted with countless sparkling stars.

Tomorrow was the trial. Her trial. She'd kept her promise to Peyton to stay out of trouble and not bother him, but she had missed seeing him and couldn't help wondering if he'd been out with Donna Fields every night.

Even though Pattie Rand had assured Tallie that Donna was not her competition, Tallie wasn't so certain. Even if Donna and Peyton weren't in love, it didn't mean they wouldn't get married. People married for all kinds of reasons, and not always for love.

Tallie removed the box of hot-chocolate mix from the cupboard, filled a red ceramic mug with tap water and placed it in the microwave. Even if she and Peyt weren't meant to be together, it didn't mean she didn't want him to be happy, to love and be loved.

A tight knot of pain formed in Tallie's stomach at the thought of Peyt in love with another woman. Oh, she knew there had been other women in his life, plenty of women, but he'd never been in love with any of them. She supposed that somewhere in the back of her mind, she'd always hoped that someday he'd look at her and realize that he loved her the way she loved him.

Yeah, sure, Tallie. When pigs fly! Besides, you're better off without Peyt. The man is a control freak, a real bossy-butt and know-it-all. As nothing more than your friend, he tries to run your life. He thinks you're wasting your life working at the garage with Mike instead of going back to college for a degree.

"But he doesn't understand that college bored me to death, that I love trucks and cars, owning my own business, being my own boss," Tallie said out loud in the stillness of her kitchen.

The microwave beeper sounded. Removing the mug, Tallie mixed the chocolate with the hot water and stirred the contents until it was smooth. She pulled out one of the white chairs from the table and sat down on the red-checked cushion adorning the seat. Taking a sip of her hot cocoa, Tallie sighed.

Peyton Rand. Their paths really never should have crossed. If the Senator hadn't been a hunter and fisherman, the Rand brothers wouldn't have met Claude Bishop's grandchildren. Tallie's brothers wouldn't have become close friends with Peyt and Spence. Tallie never would have got a teenage crush on the handsome elder Rand son, the one who always took time to pay attention to the tagalong little sister.

She had made such a fool of herself when she'd been sixteen and professed her undying love for Peyt. He'd been unbelievably kind when he rejected her, assuring her that someday she'd really fall in love and the man she loved would be the luckiest guy on earth.

Tallie laughed. Tears gathered in the corners of her eyes. *Dammit, stop that,* she chided herself. There are more serious matters to concern you than the fact that Peyton Rand isn't in love with you. Tomorrow you're going on trial for shooting Cliff Nolan.

Sheba entered the room, Solomon not far behind her. The gray tabby curled herself around Tallie's leg, a soothing caress as if in sympathy. "Yeah, Sheba, I did it this time, didn't I? Of course, it should help matters that Cliff was kicking around Richie and Whitey and that he didn't even have to stay overnight in the hospital when Doc Hall finished picking out that birdshot."

Solomon looked at Tallie, his big brown eyes surveying her with what she knew was understanding. Tallie believed that animals possessed a sixth sense when it came to people, that they were in tune with the humans who loved them.

"You know me better than anyone, don't you, Sol? You know I'm scared, and you know I'm afraid that after the trial, Peyt really will wash his hands of me."

She wasn't sure which worried her the most, the possibility of actually going to jail or the threat that this time Peyt finally had gotten enough and would walk away from her and never look back.

Tallie raised the mug to her lips. The telephone rang. She glanced at the clock on the stove. Eleven-fifteen. Who would be calling at this time of night? Mike was on tow-truck duty this week.

The phone continued ringing while Tallie made her way into the living room. She picked up the receiver off the wooden corner desk.

"Hello."

"Tallie, this is Loretta Nolan." The woman's voice trembled. "Please . . . please help me."

"What's wrong, Loretta? Has Cliff hurt you again?"

"I . . . I'm ready to leave him, Tallie. Please . . . oh, dear God, please . . ."

Tallie clutched the phone with white-knuckled ferocity. "Is he there? Does he know you're calling me? Are you and the kids safe?"

"He's been here...and...gone. The kids are okay. Just scared." Tallie could hear the tears in Loretta's voice. "He gave me a black eye and busted my lip, but I'm okay."

"You get whatever you want to take packed, and I'll be over to pick y'all up as soon as I can."

"Tallie, I ain't never coming back to him. He...he threatened to... I'm afraid for the kids." Loretta's voice broke on a choked sob.

"It'll be all right. I'm on my way." Tallie hung up the receiver and rushed through the house into her bedroom.

Thank you, Lord. Thank you for making Loretta see the light before Cliff killed her or one of those precious children.

Tallie jerked off her robe and sleep-shirt, then pulled on a pair of jeans and an oversize, long-sleeved plaid shirt. While slipping into a pair of tennis shoes, she suddenly remembered her promise to Peyton. She'd promised him that she'd stay out of trouble.

But this wasn't her trouble; it was Loretta's. Would Peyton understand? Would he be upset that the night before her trial, the trial for shooting Cliff Nolan, she was helping the man's wife and children escape from him? Surely, Peyton would understand. He couldn't want Loretta to continue living with a man who made her every waking moment a never-ending nightmare?

Once dressed, Tallie returned to the telephone in the living room, dialed the number she knew by heart and waited.

"Hello?" Peyton said.

"Peyt, this is Tallie. I'm sorry to bother you so late, but...well...I have a slight problem."

"It's less than twelve hours until your trial starts," Peyton told her. "Couldn't you solve this problem on your own without involving me?"

"Of course I can!"

"Then why call me?"

"Because I promised you I'd stay out of trouble, and I thought it only right for me to call and warn you that what I plan to do tonight might create more problems for me with Cliff Nolan." Tallie came close to hanging up at that precise moment, but she knew it would only infuriate Peyt, and she needed him on her side in that courtroom come morning.

"What are you planning to do tonight?"

"I'm on my way over to pick up Loretta Nolan and her children. She's finally come to her senses. She's leaving Cliff, and she wants my help."

"Good God!"

"There's nothing you can say that will stop me. So don't waste your breath."

"Is Cliff Nolan at home?" Peyton asked. "Will you be running into him when you go over there?"

"Loretta said he was gone."

"Then go get her and the children right now. Bring them back to your house. I'll be there as soon as possible."

"Are you saying . . . do you mean you approve?"

"Keep your doors locked. Keep Solomon on alert and have your shotgun loaded. Do you hear me, Tallie? This is going to infuriate Nolan."

"There's no need for you to drive all the way here from Jackson tonight—"

"Tallie, I'll make a few phone calls. Loretta needs to be in a safe house, somewhere Cliff can't find her."

Tallie nodded, then realized Peyt couldn't see her. "All right. There's a place in Marshallton."

"You go get Loretta and the children. I'll make arrangements from my car phone on the way to meet you."

Tallie wished Peyton were within touching distance. She'd throw her arms around him and kiss the living daylights out of him. "Thank you. You're one in a million. You know that, don't you?"

"So are you, Tallie. So are you."

* * *

Peyton stood in the doorway, darkness from the long corridor behind him. Only a dim light from the lone lamp illuminated the small room where Loretta Nolan tucked her two younger children into a half-bed. Richie Nolan, tall and reed-thin, stared at Tallie, his pointed little chin trembling as he held back tears.

"Y'all will be safe here," Tallie said. "I'll call every day, but I won't come around for a while, just in case Cliff tries to follow me."

"Thank you." Loretta still knelt beside the bed where her hand rested atop the covers sheltering her babies from the cool night air. "I should have listened to you a long time ago, Tallie. If I had..."

Tallie gazed into Loretta's moist blue eyes, all the while trying desperately to avoid staring at the bruises on her face or the dried blood on her lip. Tension coiled inside Tallie, a fierce anger at the cruelty one human being could inflict on another. How could a man harm the woman he claimed to love?

"The past doesn't matter." Tallie took a deep breath, then tried to smile. The effort created a gripping pain at the top of her throat.

"I'll never forget what you and Mr. Rand have done for me and my kids." Loretta pulled herself to her feet, wincing when she put weight on her left leg.

"You don't owe us anything, Mrs. Nolan." Peyton slipped his arm around Tallie's waist. "But you do owe yourself and your children a better life. The people here can help you, and so will Tallie and I, in any way we can."

"I'll be in touch soon." Tallie could not resist the temptation to lean against Peyton, to rest her weary body against the solid strength of his powerful frame. Dear Lord, what would she do without him?

Running the few feet across the room, Richie threw his arms around Tallie, clinging to her legs. "I love you, Tallie. I love you for stopping Daddy from hurting me and Whitey." Tears streamed down the child's heart-shaped face. "You…you take care of Whitey for me. He's a good dog."

Peyton released his hold on Tallie. Dropping to a squat, she reached out and wiped the tears from Richie's eyes with her fingertips. "I'll make sure Whitey is taken care of, don't you worry." Tallie promised herself that she would find Richie's dog a loving home.

Loretta walked over, pulled her son away from Tallie and circled his frail body with her thin arms. Mother and son looked at Tallie, their tired, haggard expressions brightening with gratitude. "If I'm needed to testify tomorrow, I'll come to the courthouse," Loretta said.

"No, you musn't do that." Tallie hadn't once given a thought to Loretta testifying against her husband. "You hadn't planned on calling her as a witness, had you, Peyt?"

"I think we can handle the situation without you, Mrs. Nolan. It will be better for you if your husband has no idea where you and the children are." Peyton felt fairly certain that in Clayburn Proctor's court, Tallie Bishop's word against Cliff Nolan's would be sufficient defense.

Peyton touched Tallie's back. She tensed. When he leaned down to whisper in her ear, she shuddered.

"Let's go. Let Mrs. Nolan and the children settle in." Peyton slid his hand down to Tallie's waist and gave her a gentle nudge.

Tallie took one final glimpse, forcing a goodbye smile on her lips. Without looking back, she allowed Peyton to lead her out into the hallway. Once the door closed behind them and they'd made their way almost to the front door, Tallie pulled away from Peyton and leaned her head against the wall. Tears welled up inside her. Her slender shoulders shook.

Peyton felt her pain. He couldn't bear to see Tallie suffering, and this tenderhearted, sentimental female took all the hurts of the world into her own soul. If only everyone cared the way Tallie did, there would be no injustices in this world and the only agonies would be the kinds beyond human control.

He took her shoulders in his strong grasp, pulling her ever so slowly away from the wall, turning her until her bowed head rested on his chest. Damn, but she was tiny. The top of her curly dark head rested on his breastbone. He tilted her chin upward, making her face him. Tears moistened her warm brown eyes and dampened her soft pink cheeks.

He wanted to kiss away her tears. "Don't cry, sugar. Everything is going to be all right."

Sighing deeply, Tallie slipped her arms around Peyton's waist, savoring the feel of his hard chest beneath her head, the rapid rise and fall as he breathed in and out, the steady beat of his heart. "Why, Peyt? Just tell me why? How can anyone inflict pain on anyone else, least of all someone they claim to love? A wife? A child? A helpless animal? I don't understand."

Peyton rubbed her back, soothing her as he pulled her into a close embrace. "I don't know. Psychiatrists would say that abuse is a vicious cycle. That it's learned behavior. Cliff Nolan was probably abused himself."

"Then how on earth could he..." Tallie trembled, the shivers starting slowly in her hands and gradually spreading through her entire body. "I shot him, Peyt. I filled that man's backside full of birdshot. I inflicted pain on him."

"Come on, sugar, let's get out of here. I'm taking you home, now."

Half leading, half dragging her, Peyton escorted Tallie out into the cool, damp night, then into the warmth and security of his sleek, dark blue Jag. He checked her seat belt once he got behind the steering wheel. She sat in the bucket seat, her head resting against the cushioned back, her eyes closed. Peyton reached out, his hand hovering over her.

Then he ran his fingertips down her cheek. She opened her eyes and looked at him. He stared down into liquid brown pools of temptation, eyes that spoke volumes, eyes that beckoned him to partake of forbidden fruit. He leaned closer. Tallie closed her eyes.

Damn, he wanted to kiss her. Peyton jerked away, inserted the key into the ignition and started his car. What the hell did he think he was doing? He had never taken advantage of the way Tallie felt about him, and he sure wasn't going to start now. Especially not when she was so very, very vulnerable.

When the engine roared to life, Tallie's eyelids shot open. What had happened? She'd been so sure Peyton was going to kiss her. She stared at him in the semidarkness, streaks of illumination hitting his face from the streetlights they raced past on their way out of Marshallton. Peyton's gaze focused on the windshield, his profile a hard, chiseled line in the shadows, his jaw set tightly, his big body rigid.

Tallie desperately wanted to reach out and touch him, to ease the tension she could see and feel. But she didn't dare touch him and risk his icy glare, his cold words of rejection. She watched him as they rode along the highway, both of them completely silent.

Peyt was beautifully masculine—from his deep-set blue eyes to his long, tapered nose, his wide, thin lips to his sharply squared jaw and the narrow cleft that cut his chin in half.

Oh, yes, Peyton Rand was totally male. A modern warrior in a suit instead of loincloth or shining armor. Tall and broad-shouldered with a muscular lankiness reminiscent of Old West cowboys. But Peyt was no cowboy, no rugged man of the earth. He was as sleek and elegant as the car he drove, with as much power contained inside him as the Jag's engine possessed. Peyt was a man accustomed to wealth and all the privileges that wealth afforded. He had been raised in the midst of great political and social power.

He knew the rules by which those in control of the world lived, and he was an expert at playing the game. Men feared Peyton Rand; women adored him.

Tallie Bishop adored him. Since the first time she'd laid eyes on him, she'd considered him her secret love. And in all the years since, that one fact hadn't changed. But he could never be hers. She could never exist in his world, live by his rules, change herself into an obedient, politically correct wife.

Even if Peyt could learn to love her, even if he wanted her as his life's mate, she couldn't marry Peyt. Tallie was who she was, and she couldn't change—she didn't want to change. A woman with her background and her own set of values and morals would never fit in the superficial, favor-swapping, ass-kissing kingdom in which Peyton Rand was a young prince.

Tears lodged in Tallie's throat. She turned her head sharply, not sure she could control her emotions. And she didn't want Peyt to see her crying again. She'd leaned on him too much tonight. He probably thought she was the silliest, weakest, most sniveling female he'd ever known.

Swallowing the knot of emotion choking her, Tallie stole a glimpse of Peyt. He kept his eyes glued to the road. Tallie looked away, then quickly glanced back at him. His light tan suit was slightly wrinkled, the jacket unbuttoned and hanging free on each side of his broad chest. His mauve linen shirt was buttoned all the way to the top, but he wore no tie. His appearance bespoke a casual elegance few men could ever achieve. How could the man look so incredibly gorgeous in the middle of the night?

Turning her head slightly, Tallie gazed out the side window, staring into the blackness of the night, seeking solace from a world she could not understand and from a man she dare not love.

Peyton wanted to strike out at someone or something. He clutched the steering wheel tenaciously. This was an intolerable situation, one he'd thought he could control—one he *had* controlled for quite some time. He wasn't sure when he'd first realized he wanted Tallie Bishop. It wasn't something that had struck him like a bolt of lightning; instead, it had sneaked up on him and he'd been powerless to stop it.

For the last few years, he'd found her more and more attractive every time he'd seen her, which was fairly often since she seemed to constantly be getting herself into some sort of trouble. But his common sense and survival instincts had kept him away from her—emotionally and sexually.

In his mind, and even once on paper, he had listed all the reasons that would make it disastrous for the two of them to have an affair. First, Tallie was ten years younger than he was, and he was a good friend to all three of her older brothers. Jake, Hank and Caleb would take turns beating him to a pulp if he ever deliberately broke Tallie's heart. Then there was the indisputable fact that he and Tallie came from two very different worlds and lived two totally opposing life-styles. He knew himself and he knew Tallie well enough to realize neither of them was likely to change. Besides, would he really want Tallie to change? No. Part of her attraction was her free-hearted, loving nature. Tallie had the soul of an empathist—a woman capable of experiencing the pain of others. And heaven help her, Tallie couldn't bear to see people or animals in pain and not try to alleviate that pain.

She had filled Cliff Nolan with birdshot to stop him from abusing his son and the child's dog. But that softhearted soul of hers wept with remorse at having caused Nolan pain. Peyton wondered if he'd ever been sorry for anything he'd done. Oh, not little things, but some of the big decisions that had affected his life and the lives of others. He had always been a man of action, but that action was always taken after considerable deliberation, weighing all sides of an issue. And once he'd acted upon his decision, he seldom looked back. He wasn't a man filled with regrets.

Except one. He regretted that he couldn't make love to Tallie Bishop.

Solomon and Whitey met them in the driveway when Peyton stopped the Jag in front of Tallie's house. The front-porch light revealed Sheba lying on the wooden swing, nonchalantly licking her little paws.

Neither Peyton nor Tallie made a move to exit the car. Turning slowly, Peyton looked at her. She raised her head and met his stare head-on.

"Thanks for your help tonight," Tallie said. "And your understanding."

"You'd better get some rest. The trial starts at ten in the morning." He knew he should open the door, get out and assist Tallie in a gentlemanly fashion, then say good-night and get the hell away from her as fast as he could.

But he couldn't. His desire to be with her, to look at her, to smell that fresh, clean fragrance of pure Tallie compelled him to draw out their time together.

"I guess it's pretty late." Tallie felt her wrist. It was bare. In her haste to help Loretta, she'd forgotten to put on her watch.

Turning on the interior lighting, Peyton checked his Rolex. "Damn, it's after three."

"I'd better go on in."

"Yeah. Come morning, we're both going to look and feel like hell."

"I don't think I'll be able to sleep." She looked at him, unable to stop herself, knowing that her eyes issued an invitation and a plea.

He ran his long fingers through his thick blond hair. "Me, neither."

"You...you could come in for coffee. I've got decaf." Idiot, she chided herself. Don't do this to yourself. You're practically begging him to come inside and stay with you.

"Coffee would be great." What sort of fool are you, man? You've steered clear of situations that put you alone with this woman, and here you are ready to walk into her house in the middle of the night. Coffee isn't all she's offering, and coffee isn't all you want.

Tallie turned on light after light as she walked through her house from living room to kitchen. Peyton followed, sensing with each step the nervous tension coming from Tallie. He glanced idly at the living room as they passed through. Clean, homey, but slightly cluttered. He had the urge to start picking up items off the floor.

"Come on in and sit down. The coffee won't take long to brew fresh, or we can drink instant." She felt like kicking her own behind for asking him in, for issuing an invitation she was sure to regret.

"How about the real stuff?" He reached out to touch her shoulder, thought better of it and dropped his hand. "We can talk about the trial while we're waiting. Go over a few crucial points again."

Peyton pulled out a white wooden chair and sat down on the red-checked cushion. The room had been redecorated and somewhat modernized since Claude Bishop's death. The walls and appliances were pristine white and a row of windows opened up a view of the backyard and nearby woods.

Like the living room, the kitchen possessed a clean yet cluttered appearance. It was obvious that Tallie really lived in her house.

Peyton wasn't sure he'd ever *lived* anywhere. In his father's house, his grandmother Rand had run their home with the precision of a headmistress in a boarding school. He and Spence and their older sister Valerie had had set bedtimes and wakeup times, even on weekends. Toys were played with one at a time and always put away neatly. Loud music was forbidden. Loud noise, even roughhousing fun with Spence, had been taboo. Food was served in the dining room by servants. Peyton had no memories of ever having eaten in the kitchen during his grandmother's lifetime.

Peyton's apartment had been decorated by an interior designer he'd dated years ago. She'd told him that it reflected his personality. If it did, he was a colorless, cold, black-and-white guy. Every stick of furniture was sleek, lean and ultramodern. And nothing was out of place. No clutter, no dirty dishes in the sink, no wet towels on the floor, no crumbs on the table.

Peyton Rand liked his life orderly. His mind functioned best when he had control over every aspect in his world.

As if on cue, reminding him that Tallie Bishop was one aspect over which he would never have any control, she pulled out a chair and sat down opposite him.

"I've got some fried peach pies. Would you like one to go with the coffee?" She didn't want to talk about the trial. She didn't even want to discuss what the future would hold for Loretta Nolan and her children. No, all Tallie wanted was to fall into Peyton's arms and ask him to hold her.

She could never remember being held. Oh, Grandpa Claude was a good-hearted man, but not overly affectionate, and he'd always treated her just like her brothers, as if she were just another boy. Jake and Hank and Caleb had loved her dearly and been protective big brothers, but they hadn't known the first thing about how to treat a girl. They, too, had grown up without any female influence in their lives.

Sometimes, Tallie desperately needed to be hugged, to be held close and soothed. Occasionally, a friend—Sheila or Susan—would give her a sisterly, affectionate hug, but those kinds of hugs weren't enough anymore. Tallie wanted and needed the loving, tender passion of a man.

She needed Peyton Rand to love her. But he didn't.

"Fried peach pies?" Peyton asked. "I know you didn't make them. If I recall, your cooking skills weren't any better than your brothers'."

"I most certainly did make them." Tallie relaxed slightly, the tightness in her muscles easing. "Sheila's been teaching me how to cook for several years now."

"Are they edible?"

"My peach pies? Of course they're edible, but I'm not sure I'll let you have some now."

Peyton laughed, the tension draining out of him like melted butter dripping from a hot biscuit. Without thinking, he reached across the table and took Tallie's hand. She flinched, then stiffened. He ran his thumb over the top of her hand, caressing her knuckles.

"Don't worry about the trial tomorrow and don't worry about Loretta Nolan." Peyton took Tallie's hand in his. "Everything is going to turn out all right."

"Is it, Peyt?"

Tallie's question stunned him. He knew only too well that she wasn't referring only to the trial and Loretta Nolan, but to the future—their future.

"I think that after the trial, you and I need to discuss things."

"Why don't we discuss things right now?"

Peyton wasn't ready to cut the ties that bound him to Tallie. Not yet. Not tonight. But for both their sakes, he would have to sever those ties, after the trial. Neither of them could go on the way they'd been going. Their desire for each other was hurting them both.

"After the trial will be soon enough. I'll take you out for dinner and when I bring you home, we'll have our little talk."

Tallie couldn't bring herself to look him in the eye. She was too afraid he'd see her pain and know how much she loved him. After the trial, he was going to cut her free, and thus free himself from the burden of their relationship.

Tallie glanced at the coffeemaker. Enough hot, black decaf for two cups filled the glass pot. "Ready for coffee?"

Not waiting for his reply, she jumped up and busied herself with preparations, then set a cup in front of Peyt and took the other herself. When she sat down, she raised her cup in a toast. "Here's to tomorrow night, after the trial. To ending something that never should have started in the first place." Tears floated in her eyes. She swallowed. Her hands trembled, shaking the cup she clutched.

"Tallie..." He looked at her and wished he hadn't. She was on the verge of tears. "Nothing ever really started between us, you know. Just friendship, of a sort. Brotherly concern on my part. A teenage crush on yours."

Tallie set her cup on the table, coffee sloshing over the sides, staining the white surface with dark splotches. She slid back her chair, standing with her back to Peyt, her gaze focused on some unseen spot in the backyard. "Asking you in for coffee was a bad idea. You agreed because you didn't want to hurt my feelings, didn't you?"

"No, Tallie, that's not true."

"Oh, yes...it...is." Her voice broke on an emotional sigh. She was not going to fall apart and start crying. Not yet. Not until after Peyt left. "You've been looking out for me for years now. Not because you wanted to, but because you felt it was something you had to do. Out of friendship to my brothers. Out of concern for me because I can't seem to stay out of trouble."

"Tallie..."

Her shoulders trembled with the force of her unshed tears. "I could have taken care of myself without your help, you know. I don't need you coming to my rescue, so after the trial, I'll never call on you again."

"Tallie, this is not the time—"

"All right. We'll play by your rules. We always do. We'll wait."

Peyton stood, walked over to Tallie and reached out to take her shoulders in his strong hands. He hesitated. Don't touch her! his good judgment shouted. But she's hurting, and I'm the one who hurt her, his heart replied. Grasping her shoulders, he turned her toward him. She looked down at the floor, trying to avoid any direct eye contact.

"Look at me, Tallie."

"Go home. Leave me alone." She tried to pull away from him, but he held fast.

"Don't do this to yourself, sugar. Don't do this to me."

Her gaze flew upward, staring at him, unsure of what she saw in his expression. "What am I doing to you?"

"You're making me crazy."

"I'm—"

Quickly, totally disregarding any warnings his mind issued, Peyton cut off her reply by covering her mouth with his. Stunned by the unexpected urgency of his kiss, Tallie didn't respond at first; then when he deepened the kiss, thrusting his tongue inside and jerking her into his arms so close that her breasts crushed into his chest, she gave in to the wild, hot sweetness spreading through her.

For one brief moment, she realized that Peyt was kissing her the way she'd always dreamed he would, and then her mind gave way to her senses and she didn't think at all. She simply felt.

With the same quick certainty with which he'd kissed her, Peyton released her and drew away, staring at her as if he couldn't believe what had happened. Her own expression mirrored his.

"That shouldn't have happened," he said.

When she didn't respond, he drew in a deep breath and shook his head slightly, as if to clear his thoughts. "Be at the courthouse by nine-thirty. I'll be waiting for you, and we'll go over everything briefly before the trial."

When he started to leave the kitchen, Tallie followed. He stopped, but didn't turn around. "I'll see myself out."

Tallie stood silently, watching him walk out of her kitchen. Tomorrow, after the trial, he would walk out of her life. And there was nothing she could do about it. Not unless she was willing to change her whole life, to become someone she wasn't.

She couldn't do that. Not even for Peyton Rand.

Four

Tallie let out a sigh of relief. The room burst into thunderous applause, resounding shouts and cries of happiness as friends and acquaintances rose to their feet. Wielding his gavel, Judge Clayburn Proctor called for order in his courtroom.

Without giving her actions a second thought, Tallie threw her arms around Peyton, hugging him fiercely, thanking him again and again as camera flashes exploded all around them and newspaper reporters crowded closer.

Tallie's own personal thoughts and emotions drowned out the wild uproar bombarding her ears. She wasn't going to jail for shooting Cliff Nolan with birdshot. Judge Proctor had found her guilty of a misdemeanor, given her a stiff fine and then warned her not to repeat such a thoughtless action again. Relief flooded her body, her mind and her heart. She knew that, in part, she owed her freedom not only to the benevolent judge, but to the persuasive arguments Peyton had given in explanation of her behavior.

"It's all over," Peyton told her as he pulled her arms from around his neck and shoved her away from him with gentle force.

She gazed up at him, into his deep blue eyes, and knew he meant that more than just the trial was over. Their relationship was over. After today, she wouldn't be seeing Peyton again. It was for the best. She knew that as well as he did.

After all, she thought, just look around at all these reporters, and not all of them local as she had hoped. Even Nashville and Memphis newspapers had sent people to cover the headline news that Peyton Rand was defending a female tow-truck driver on charges of shooting a man with birdshot. This wasn't exactly the kind of case on which Peyton had built his reputation.

"I'll see the fine is taken care of," Peyton said, gripping her by the elbow as he picked up his briefcase. "Come on, let's get out of here."

"I can take care of my own fine, thank you." When she tried to jerk away from him, he tightened his grip on her, circling her arm with his hand.

"You don't have that much cash money, Tallie, and I know it. Consider it a loan. You can mail monthly payments to my office." Pulling her close to his side, he maneuvered her forward, making his way through the crowd. "Don't argue. Let's just get the hell away from this three-ring circus. I promised you dinner after the trial, didn't I?"

"There's no need for that. Sheila brought me in to Marshallton this morning, and I can get her to take me home. Her or Mike. They're both here."

"Looks like most of Crooked Oak is here." If Peyton had ever doubted Tallie's popularity in her little home-town, the support she had received today would have erased that doubt.

As she and Peyt passed by, Tallie glanced over to where a cleanly shaved and uncharacteristically sober Cliff Nolan sat beside assistant district attorney, Marsha Hunt. The man glared at her, his bloodshot eyes boring into her like poison daggers. A foreboding chill racked Tallie's body.

Reporters swarmed over them as they tried to push their way through the throng of well-wishers. Tallie couldn't see over anyone's head, but she did make out the lavender stripes on Sheila's skirt only a few inches away.

"Tell us, Mr. Rand, why an attorney of your status would take on a case like this?" a gray-haired, bespectacled reporter asked.

"Is it true that Ms. Bishop is a personal friend of yours, that the two of you have been involved since she was a teenager?" A Yankee-accented female TV reporter thrust a microphone in Peyton's face.

Peyton's deadly stare swept over the attractive young woman, whose smile faded but whose hand continued holding out the mike.

Without answering any of the questions hurled at him, Peyton led Tallie forward, one slow, agonizing step at a time. Leaning down to accommodate her shorter height, he told her to ignore the reporters. Easy for him, maybe, but she wasn't used to being the center of media attention.

"Ms. Bishop, is it true that this isn't the first time Mr. Rand has come to your rescue? That indeed the two of you are intimately involved?" a dashing, young black reporter asked.

Tallie opened her mouth to deny the man's accusation, but closed it again when Peyton squeezed her elbow. How could he endure this? she wondered. She'd had no idea that his defending her would create such a ruckus. She'd been fairly certain the local Marshallton paper would send over a reporter, but the horde of media assaulting them was something she most definitely hadn't expected.

Lowell Redman stood just outside the courtroom door, looking quite distinguished in his sheriff's uniform. He waved at Peyton, motioning them in his direction. Tallie heard him speaking, but couldn't make out what he'd said. The racket coming from both reporters and well-wishers was almost deafening as the people followed them out into the corridor.

Without questioning his move, Tallie followed Peyton down the corridor, through a door marked Private, down a hallway and a flight of stairs. The door closed behind them. No one followed.

"Where are we going?" Tallie finally asked when Peyton slowed down enough for her to catch her breath.

"Lowell is guarding the door to give us a chance to escape out the back way. They bring prisoners in and out this way."

"So we're going outside?"

"Lowell had my car brought around to the back entrance. If we hurry, we might get away before the reporters figure out where we've gone."

"I've never seen anything like it. All those reporters. And their questions! They made it sound as if you and I . . . that we're—"

"Lovers? Yeah, I know."

"That's not good for your reputation, is it? To be linked with someone like me."

Peyton flung open the door. Late-afternoon sunshine greeted them, a warm breeze swirling around, teasing Tallie's short black hair.

"Looks like the coast is clear," he said. "There's my Jag."

Tallie noticed the dark blue car parked only a few feet away. "I need to tell Sheila where I'm going, that I won't be riding home with her."

"Lowell will take care of that."

Just as Peyton and Tallie made a mad dash from the courthouse to his car, Cliff Nolan stepped out from behind a row of tall shrubbery alongside the police and sheriff's parking area.

"Where's Loretta? What have you done with my wife and my kids?" Cliff shouted. "I know you done talked her into leaving me."

Tallie froze to the spot beside the Jag, her hand hovering over the door handle. How had Cliff made his way outside so quickly? How had he known where she and Peyton would exit? Then she remembered that Cliff had been a prisoner of the local authorities more than once and probably knew the courthouse like the back of his hand.

"Your wife and children are safe, Nolan. They're where you can never harm them again." Peyton glanced from Nolan to Tallie, who seemed incapable of speech or movement.

"This is all your fault, Tallie Bishop." Cliff took several steps forward, then stopped when he looked at Peyton. "You got her off scot-free today, didn't you, Mr. Big-Shot Lawyer, but you can't watch her every minute of every day."

As suddenly as her voice and motion had failed her, they returned. Tallie bounded around the side of the Jag. "Don't you try to scare me with your threats, Cliff Nolan. I'm not afraid of you. You don't scare me the way you did Loretta. I've got a dog and I've got a gun. Don't think I'll ever let you hurt me."

"Sooner or later, I'll pay you back. Not just for the birdshot—" he rubbed his backside "—but for taking away my family, for turning them against me."

"If you ever harm Tallie, I'll—"

"Like I said, Mr. Rich-and-Famous Rand, you ain't going to be with her twenty-four hours a day. She's going to pay for what she's done to me and mine."

Before Peyton could respond, a bevy of reporters rounded the side of the courthouse, storming toward Peyton and Tallie with the force of a hurricane.

"Get in the car! Now!" Peyton said.

Tallie obeyed instantly, realizing that their immediate threat wasn't Cliff Nolan, but the unrelenting press corps with their insinuations and accusations.

Peyton's Jag roared to life. With the ease of a man who had escaped reporters before, Peyton sped out of the parking area and onto the main street, heading the car away from downtown.

"Will they follow us?" Tallie asked.

"If they had any idea where we're going, they would. Some of them will probably show up at your house in a little while. Others will stake out my apartment for a few hours."

"You're kidding?"

"I only wish I were." Peyton glanced in his rearview mirror, breathing a sigh of relief when he didn't see any cars following.

"All of that—" she nodded back toward the general direction of the courthouse "—was because of who you are. A Rand. A Rand who's considering running for governor."

"People want to know all the intimate details of their politicians' lives. Even potential politicians."

Hugging herself, Tallie shivered. "I've really made a mess for you this time, haven't I?"

Peyton drove the Jag along several back streets, maneuvering it toward the outskirts of town, toward the main highway leading to Mississippi. He'd made reservations for dinner at a catfish restaurant a good hour's drive from Crooked Oak. He'd had a pretty good idea what would happen after the trial. He wanted privacy and quiet tonight when he discussed his decision with Tallie...when he told her that he wasn't going to see her again. "I'll clear everything up tomorrow."

"How can you do that?"

"I'll issue a statement."

Turning in her seat, Tallie stared at Peyton. So cool and controlled in his navy-blue suit, his gray-, blue- and white-striped tie, his Italian leather shoes and his eighteen-karat-gold Rolex. "What sort of statement?"

"One to the effect that I've been a family friend for years, ever since my father and your grandfather became hunting and fishing buddies."

"In other words, you're going to tell them the truth and expect them to believe it?" Shaking her head, Tallie grunted. "Those people are out for blood. Your blood. They're not going to accept the truth."

"They'll have no choice but to believe me, since after tonight, you and I won't be seen together again."

There it was, she thought. The truth she'd been dreading. Peyton really was going to end things tonight. He was going to say goodbye, walk out of her life and never look back.

Well, what had she expected? She'd known there was no chance for them, that they were as ill suited as any two people could possibly be. Their relationship should have ended long ago. If it had, maybe she would have moved on with her life. Maybe she would have found someone else to love, instead of holding on to hopeless dreams.

"Where are you taking me?" Tallie asked, her gaze riveted to the evening sun making its way downward in the western sky.

"To Tommy Tubbs's catfish house down in Mississippi. Nobody will know us there, and Tommy's expecting us. He'll serve us dinner at a nice secluded table where we can have privacy."

"Privacy for our little talk?"

Peyton didn't fool himself. He knew Tallie was well aware of what he wanted to talk to her about tonight. Calling a halt to their relationship was the best thing for her as well as for him. So why was it that he felt like such a heel? Because, he told himself, you're afraid you're acting just like the Senator, putting yourself and your career before everyone else.

The one person on earth Peyton didn't want to emulate was his father, but, try as he might, he could not escape the similarities in their personalities, their physical appearance or their political aspirations. His father had presented a Southern-gentleman facade to the world, but underneath, Marshall Rand had been a ruthless, self-centered, hypocritical bastard. Every day of his life, Peyton had fought against those qualities, ever aware of the disastrous effect his father had on other people's lives, especially the lives of his own children.

Peyton stole a quick glance at Tallie and his heart skipped a beat. He didn't think he'd ever seen her in a dress. The one she wore was a simple, inexpensive, off-the-rack little number that most of the women he dated never would have purchased. But it suited Tallie, an unadorned, short-sleeved, scooped-neck dress in a buttercup yellow, with a straight skirt that clung to Tallie's rounded hips.

"Why don't you relax? The trial's over. Loretta and her children are in a safe house. Everything is going to be all right."

"I can take a hint," Tallie said. "You changed the subject because you don't want to give me the brush-off until after we've eaten dinner."

Despite the worry eating away at his insides, Peyton laughed. Tallie Bishop had to be the most honest, straight-to-the-point woman he'd ever known.

"I'm not giving you the brush-off."

Tallie snorted. Peyton grinned.

"Okay," she said. "Call it what you will. You're dumping me tonight, and we both know it."

"Don't be so melodramatic. You and I have never been lovers or sweethearts. We've never even dated. So how could I give you the brush-off or dump you or whatever *you* want to call it?"

"Don't cloud the issue with technicalities. You know damn well what I mean!" Crossing her arms over her chest, Tallie slumped down in the seat.

"Ladies don't say damn."

"I'm not a lady, and you damn well know it."

"Okay. Okay. Even if you're ready for a confrontation, I'm not. I went into court today without any sleep. I got a guilty client off practically scot-free, and I had to face a mob of nosy reporters. I'd like a couple of hours to relax before I have to face any more problems."

"And that's exactly what I am, aren't I? I'm a problem. That's all I am to you. All I've ever been."

Peyton made no response. Tallie noticed the visible tensing in his shoulders, the stern tightening of his facial muscles. All right, she thought, what difference did it make? If they confronted the inevitable now or a few hours from now, the end result would be the same. Peyton Rand was cutting her out of his life.

Tallie sat down in the porch swing, patted the blue-and-white striped cushion, then nudged the swing into action with a swift push on the wooden floor.

"Sit down beside me," she said. "I don't bite."

With his hands in his pockets, Peyton stood on the edge of the porch, staring out into the darkness. "This isn't easy for me, Tallie."

"No, I don't suppose it is," she agreed. "If it were easy, you would have already gotten to it instead of putting it off as long as possible."

He turned sharply, looking directly at her. He could have told her after the trial when they were alone in his car, but he'd waited because he'd planned to tell her in the restaurant. Then after dinner, he'd tried again to tell her. She'd been willing to listen, even insistent that he get it over with, but he'd postponed saying the words. Now, he couldn't put it off any longer. Before he left her tonight, he had to tell her that their relationship was over, that they were not going to see each other again under any circumstances.

"We've known each other a long time." Why was he having so much difficulty finding the right words? He was a lawyer, an aspiring politician; diplomacy and tact were a part of his everyday life.

"Since I was thirteen," Tallie said. "That was the first time Grampa Claude let me go hunting with y'all."

"Hank was something with a rifle, wasn't he? The surest shot in these parts."

"Hank was the best sportsman, Caleb the best athlete and Jake the smartest of all of us. So, what does that have to do with what you've got to tell me tonight?"

"Nothing," Peyton admitted. "Except that I promised Caleb that I'd keep an eye on you since none of them were going to be around to do it. Your brothers have counted on me to help keep you out of trouble."

"Caleb left eight years ago, Peyt. I think you've served your time. After all, keeping an eye on me wasn't supposed to be a life sentence."

"You know things can't go on this way." Reaching inside his coat pocket, Peyton removed a cigar and a lighter. "We're in a no-win situation here."

Tallie gave the swing a harder push, then closed her eyes as she breathed in the sweet scent of the country night air and listened to the nocturnal sounds of nature.

"Regardless of what you and my brothers may think, I don't need a keeper. I'm a grown woman, and under most circumstances I can take care of myself. This trial was an exception, but you didn't have to be my lawyer. I could have hired someone else."

Peyton removed the tip from his cigar, lit it and placed it in his mouth. Taking a deep draw, he willed himself to relax. Exhaling, he turned around slowly. "It's my fault that I've allowed things to go on this long. I should have stopped coming to your aid every time you got in a jam."

Tallie shook her head. "It's just as much my fault. I didn't have to call you. I could have handled most of my problems myself. It's just that...well, I came to depend on your always being there. And...to be honest, I couldn't bear the thought of not seeing you."

Gazing down at the floor, he flicked ashes off into the yard. "Tallie—"

Stopping the swing abruptly, she stared up at Peyton. "Look, let me make this easy for you. You've spent the past eight years watching out for me as a favor to my brothers, and for eight years, I've been nothing but trouble for you. Now you've finally decided to follow in the Senator's footsteps and run for political office—governor, to be exact. Having someone like me in your life and being in politics will pose a real problem for you. So it's goodbye, Tallie, hello the governor's mansion in Nashville."

She made him feel like a real jerk, especially reminding him that he would be following in his father's footsteps. "It's not just the fact that I'm considering running for governor. There are other reasons that it would be best for us to—"

"Like the fact that I've had a crush on you since I was sixteen, that my feelings for you are an embarrassment?"

Taking another deep draw on his cigar, Peyton walked over and sat down in the swing beside Tallie. "It's not just your feelings that pose a problem for me."

She jerked around toward him, her gaze locked to his. She wasn't sure she believed what she saw in his eyes. Passion and pain, the exact feelings she knew were reflected in her own eyes.

"Are . . . are you saying that . . ."

"I'm attracted to you, Tallie. I have been for years." After one long draw on the cigar, he dropped it to the floor, crushed the smoldering tip with his foot, then kicked it out into the yard.

She swallowed hard, a distinct ringing in her ears obliterating every other sound. Sucking in a deep breath, Tallie looked down at her trembling hands resting in her lap. "Are you telling me that all these years I've been dying inside with unrequited love, you . . . you've felt the same way?"

"No." Peyton leaned over, resting his elbows on his thighs, locking his fingers in a crisscross when he dropped his hands between his legs. "Love has nothing to do with the way I feel about you."

Tallie gasped. "I see."

Peyton stole a quick glance at Tallie's pale face, the porch light casting shadows on the wall behind her. "Don't misunderstand. I care about you. I've always cared about you. But—"

"But you don't love me. I'm not the kind of woman a man like Peyton Rand could love, am I? But you can be attracted to me, can't you? Sexually attracted. You wouldn't have any problem sleeping with me, you just couldn't ever bring yourself to marry me."

"Tallie, stop talking nonsense!" He wanted to reach out, put his hands around that silky-smooth neck and strangle her. Hearing her put into words the way he felt made him sound like a heartless monster. Hell, maybe he was. Maybe he was more like his old man than even he realized.

Tallie glared at him, all the love in her heart suddenly turning into bitterness. When he reached out to touch her shoulder, she slapped his hand away. "Don't you dare touch me!"

"Tallie, listen to reason."

"If you've wanted to have sex with me, why haven't you? Lord knows I would have done anything you ever asked me to do. I've been a real fool, haven't I?" She jumped out of the swing.

Getting up, Peyton followed her to the front door, catching her hand just as she grabbed the storm-door handle. "You're not a fool, Tallie, and you're not a kid anymore, either. You're old enough to know what's been going on between us for a while now. Don't tell me you haven't felt the tension just as strongly as I have."

"I thought it was my imagination, wishful thinking on my part." She couldn't bear the feel of him so close, his hard chest against her back. Despite everything, she had the overwhelming urge to lean into him, to absorb all his masculine strength. No matter how angry and hurt she was, she still loved Peyton, and discovering that he desired her made it all the more difficult to give up the dream she'd had since she was sixteen. The dream of being Peyton Rand's woman.

Peyton pulled her hand from the handle, easing her back against him, circling her body with his arms. Tallie opened her mouth on a silent cry. The feeling of being held in his strong arms was almost more than she could bear. She had longed for this moment for years, had dreamed of the day Peyt would want her.

This was wrong, he told himself. He shouldn't be touching Tallie. Touching her was dangerous. But he couldn't stop himself. She felt so right in his arms. How long had it been since he'd wanted a woman the way he wanted Tallie? Never! He had never wanted anyone the way he wanted her.

"The last thing I want to do is hurt you," he whispered, nuzzling her ear with his nose. "I can't live your kind of life, you can't live my kind of life. You're not the type of woman who'd settle for an affair."

"How do you know what type of woman I am?" She leaned into him, snuggling closer, and at the same time trying to turn her body so that she could put her arms around him.

"You're the kind of woman who deserves more than I could ever offer." He allowed her to turn into his arms, knowing that if he didn't put a stop to their actions soon, there would be no turning back. He ached with wanting her.

She slipped her arms up and around his neck, tilted her head back and gazed into his eyes. "You haven't offered me anything. Yet."

Reaching deep within himself for his reserved will-power, Peyton took Tallie by the shoulders and shoved her gently away from him, putting enough distance between them so that their bodies didn't touch. Tallie dropped her hands to her sides.

"And I'm not going to offer you anything. Tonight I'm leaving and I'm not looking back. Don't call me, don't try to get in touch with me or see me."

"Well, you finally said it, didn't you?" Tears clogged her throat, but she held them in check. She'd be damned before she'd let him see her shed one single tear.

Still holding her by the shoulders, Peyton pulled her toward him, then stopped. "This isn't just about me, you know. I'm as bad for you as you are for me. Let's face it, sugar, we're nothing but trouble for each other."

"What would you do if I said I'd say yes if you offered me an affair?" She gave him a brave, bold look, but inside she trembled with such force she thought her knees would buckle.

He tightened his hold on her shoulders. "I can't... I'm not going to make the offer." How could a man be confronted with such temptation and not give in? How could he refuse to accept the one thing on earth he wanted most?

Caught short by what he'd just thought, Peyton wondered if he really meant it. Did he want to become Tallie's lover more than he wanted a future in politics, more than he wanted to be governor of Tennessee?

"Damn you, Tallulah!" He pulled her into his arms, jerking her up off her feet momentarily, then sliding her down his aroused body, allowing her to feel how hard he was.

"Peyt?" She clung to him, questioning and yet accepting, eager and yet afraid.

"Don't talk, sugar. Don't say anything."

His mouth covered hers with a raging hunger, hot and wild and all-consuming. He had wanted and needed and gone without for far too long. When Tallie opened her mouth with ardent anticipation, he plunged into her warmth, capturing her tongue, exploring her as his hands roamed over her back and down to her hips.

Damn, nothing had ever tasted as sweet as Tallie's warm, moist mouth. Nothing had ever felt as good as her soft body pressing into his.

He couldn't get enough of her. The musty, honeyed scent of her feminine heat surrounded him, enticing him, luring him closer and closer to the edge.

He cradled her hips in his hands while he spread kisses down her throat and onto her flesh exposed by the scooped-out neckline of her dress. "Stop me, sugar. Don't let this happen."

How could she stop him when this was what she'd longed for, what she'd dreamed of, what she'd prayed would happen? She wanted Peyton Rand. She had never wanted another man, had never given herself to anyone else, waiting and hoping that someday Peyt would become her first lover.

"I don't want to stop you," she said, clinging to him, urging him to continue.

"No promises beyond tonight," he told her, all the while lifting her into his arms, preparing to carry her inside to the nearest available bed.

Her mind heard and understood what he'd said; her heart refused to listen, building fantasies of happily-ever-after.

Just as Peyton reached out for the storm-door handle, he heard the sound of an approaching vehicle, then turned slightly in order to look down the narrow road leading to Tallie's house. Bright headlights met his gaze head-on as the thundering rattle of an old truck roared closer.

"Who is it?" Tallie asked, her arms still circling Peyton's neck, her body resting against him where he held her securely in his arms.

"I can't see. Could it be Mike?"

"His truck doesn't make that kind of noise. Besides, he's on tow-truck duty tonight."

Solomon and Whitey rounded the side of the house, both dogs barking loudly.

Peyton put Tallie on her feet, but kept his arm around her waist. The two of them took several tentative steps toward the edge of the porch. The battered truck slowed down a fraction as it approached the house, but the driver's identity was not discernible, only the fact that he was male and wore his cap pulled down, the bill obscuring the upper part of his face.

"I don't recognize the truck," Tallie said. "Maybe somebody's lost and wants directions."

Tallie pulled away from Peyt, moving toward the truck as it approached, prepared to be of assistance to the driver. But the driver didn't stop in front of her house; instead, he swerved his truck around. Peyton saw the gun in the man's hand, the porch light reflecting off the metal.

"Get back, Tallie!" Peyton shouted the moment he saw the gun was aimed in her direction.

Without giving his actions a thought, Peyton threw himself into Tallie, knocking her to the ground. The gunshots echoed in his ears as he covered Tallie's body with his own. The truck sped away, stirring up a cloud of dust.

Whitey and Solomon ran behind the departing truck, their loud barks heard distinctly over the clanking chug of the old vehicle's engine.

He lay heavily on top of her, protecting her with the armor of his body. She gave him a gentle nudge. If he didn't move soon, she wasn't going to be able to breathe.

"Peyt, I'm all right." When he didn't respond, she shoved him with a bit more force.

He rolled off her and over into the grass. Tallie rose on all fours. "Hell's toenails, Peyt, somebody just tried to shoot me!"

When Peyton's only response was a groan, Tallie leaned over him, noticing the pained expression on his face. In a panic, she ran her hands over his face, his neck and shoulders. Her quivering fingers encountered a warm, wet fluid. She jerked her hand away and held it up, seeing the dark red stain.

"Oh, dear Lord, Peyt. He shot you."

"Not too... bad," he whispered so softly Tallie barely heard him. "Call—"

"I'll call an ambulance." Tallie leaned over closer to his mouth so she could hear him better. "Are you hit anywhere else besides your shoulder?"

"Left side."

"I'll be right back," she said, forcing herself to leave him. "I'll call an ambulance and then Lowell Redman. Oh, Lordy, Peyt, who would have done such a thing?" The instant the question sprang from her mouth, two suspects came to mind. Two people ruthless enough and filled with enough hate to want to see Tallie Bishop dead. Cliff Nolan and Lobo Smothers.

If only she'd gotten a better look at the man. But it had happened so fast and it had been dark inside the truck cab.

Tallie ran into the house, making the necessary phone calls as quickly and calmly as she possibly could. Within minutes, she'd returned to Peyton's side, placing a couch pillow under his head and covering him with a crocheted throw she'd jerked off the back of her rocking chair.

"The paramedics are on their way." She sat down on the grass beside Peyton, taking his hand in hers, whispering that everything would be all right.

Whitey lay down near the porch steps. Solomon rooted his nose against Tallie's arm.

"It's all right, Sol." Tears streamed down Tallie's cheeks. "Peyt's going to be fine. Just fine."

"Don't cry, little heathen," Peyt said, squeezing her hand. "All that matters . . . is you're safe."

Tallie's heart shattered into a thousand pieces. If anything happened to Peyt, she wasn't sure she could bear to go on living.

Five

Tallie paced the floor. Having checked the wall clock every few minutes, she knew Peyton had been in surgery only an hour, but it had seemed like days. Now that he was in recovery, the waiting was almost unbearable. Although the emergency room staff had assured her Peyton's gunshot wounds were not life-threatening, she could not erase the thought from her mind that he might die. And it would be her fault. Whoever had shot Peyton had been aiming at her.

Pattie Rand placed her arm around Tallie's shoulder. "Come on and sit down for a few minutes. You're wearing me out just watching you."

"They'll send a nurse out to tell us when we can go in to see Peyt," Spence said. "My big brother wouldn't want you tearing yourself up over this. He's fine. Dr. Hall said the bullets didn't hit anything vital. No permanent damage."

Pattie led Tallie over to a green vinyl sofa, tugging her downward until she sat. "Peyton will be out of the hospital in a few days, and until he is, we can shower him with flowers and balloons and more female attention than he'll want."

"Did you call Donna Fields?" Tallie asked, knowing full well she didn't want the other woman anywhere near Peyt.

"I'll phone her in the morning." Pattie glanced at her watch. "I guess it's already morning, isn't it? I'll call her by seven, before she leaves for work."

"Maybe I should have called her right after . . . I mean if circumstances were reversed, I would have wanted her to call me." Tallie covered her face with her hands, rubbing her eyes, massaging her forehead. Then she ran her fingers through her tousled hair.

"Look, there's Lowell." Spence walked to the entrance of the surgery waiting room where Sheriff Redman stood, hat in hand.

Tallie jumped up, then stopped abruptly. Lowell had followed them to the hospital after giving specific instructions to his deputies at the crime scene. *The crime scene.* Dear Lord, the very sound of those words sent chills through Tallie.

She knew she'd been too distraught over Peyt's condition to talk sensibly to Lowell, to answer his questions coherently. All she remembered was that Spence had told her Lowell was going back to her house in Crooked Oak to make doubly sure no evidence was overlooked.

Pattie stood beside Tallie. "Are you up to answering the sheriff's questions now?"

Lowell came across the room slowly, speaking quietly to Spence as they approached Tallie. "I really need to ask you about the shooting."

Swallowing, Tallie nodded her head. "What do you want to know?"

"Can you tell me exactly what happened? What you saw? What you heard? Anything that will help us find the person who shot Peyton?"

"Come on, Tallie, sit down. You're trembling all over," Pattie said.

Pulling away from Pattie's supportive hold, Tallie walked across the room to the windows overlooking the parking area. She sucked in her cheeks, biting back the tears that threatened to overwhelm her.

"We were on the front porch," she said, her voice soft but calm. Far calmer than she felt. "We heard a truck. It was loud and noisy. I thought maybe somebody was lost and needed directions."

"The shooter drove a truck?" Lowell asked. "What kind of truck? Make? Model?"

"I'd say it was a '72 Ford. It was probably blue once, but the color had faded. There was a lot of rust, and somebody had tried to spray paint it in spots with some white paint."

"That's one of the best vehicle descriptions I've ever heard." Lowell put his hand on Tallie's shoulder. "Didn't happen to notice the license plate, did you?"

"I didn't see a tag on the truck."

"Did you get a look at the person or persons in the truck?"

Swallowing her tears, Tallie turned to face Lowell. "There was only one person in the truck. A man. A fairly big man, I think. He wore a cap with the bill pulled down over his forehead. It all happened so quickly and the only light was the porch light. It was dark inside the truck cab. I couldn't see the driver." Tallie trembled, her hands shaking so badly that she clutched them together.

"It's all right." Pattie reached out and took Tallie's hands in hers. "The worst is over. Peyton's going to be just fine."

"Did you recognize anything about the man?" Lowell asked.

"No. Nothing." Tallie held tightly to Pattie's hands. "I didn't even see the gun until it was too late. Peyt saw what was happening and shoved me out of the way."

"Are you saying that the man was trying to shoot you?"

"Yes, I think he was. Don't you see," Tallie said, "Peyt saved my life. He took the bullets that someone meant for me."

A tall, slender nurse appeared in the doorway. Her name tag read Crowler. "Is there someone here from the Rand family? Mr. Rand is awake."

Tallie rushed toward the nurse. "How is he? Is he in pain? Can I see him now?"

"Are you a member of the family?" the nurse asked.

"We're all family," Spence said, nodding toward Tallie and then Pattie.

"I'm afraid three of you can't go in at once. Perhaps two." Nurse Crowler turned, motioning for the family to follow her. "I'll take you to Mr. Rand."

"Come on, Tallie." Spence placed his open palm on Tallie's back.

"But...I...I..."

"Something tells me that you're the person Peyt wants to see," Spence said.

"If she's Tallie, then she's most definitely the person he wants to see." Nurse Crowler didn't miss a step as she led them down the hallway. "He's been calling for her ever since he regained consciousness. He seems quite concerned as to whether or not she's all right."

The tears Tallie had been able to hold in check for the past hour could no longer be contained. When they streamed down her cheeks, she brushed them away with her hand.

Peyt was worried about her. That crazy, wonderful man had risked his life to save hers, and his first thought on awakening from surgery had been about her safety. She didn't think she'd ever loved Peyton Rand more than she did at this precise moment. If only there was some way she could prove to him just how much.

Peyton lay on pristine sheets, his big body connected to a series of tubes and wires. His face appeared slightly pale, considering his tanned complexion, but his dark blue eyes were wide open and staring directly at Tallie.

She couldn't stop herself from rushing to his bedside, from leaning down and touching his face with her fingertips, from pressing her lips against his cool forehead.

"Oh, Peyt... Peyt. I..."

"Hey, sugar, you aren't going to fall apart on me, are you?" Peyton reached up and touched her hair, then speared his fingers through it, adjusting her head so that he could reach her lips. His kiss was quick and hard and filled with life.

"I'm fine, Peyt. Just fine." She glanced over at Spence. "Aren't I, Spence? I gave Lowell Redman all the information I could, and he'll find the man who shot you."

"I'd say he should start with Cliff Nolan, then check out Lobo Smothers. The guy looked a bit too big for Nolan, but I'm not sure. It was so damned dark." Peyton motioned for his brother. "Until I'm out of here and can take care of things, I want you and Pattie to keep an eye on Tallie for me."

"No problem," Spence said.

"Yes, there is a problem." Tallie pulled away from Peyton. "The last thing I want is for the Rand family to get any more involved in this situation than they already are. My God, Peyt, you're lying here with two holes in your body because I've made an enemy out there who wants to see me dead."

"All the more reason you need protection." Peyton tried to sit up.

Tallie pushed him down gently. "Don't move around. It's not good for you."

"When you leave the hospital today, I want you to go home with Spence and Pattie," Peyton said.

Tallie picked up Peyton's hand, fingering the tube leading to the IV solution hanging above the bed. "I don't want you involved in this. I can't bear the thought of your getting hurt again. Whatever's going on, I brought it on myself by interfering in somebody's business, and we both know it."

"Tallie—"

"You're not going to sacrifice any more for me. Do you understand what I'm saying?" She loved Peyton. She would not allow him to put his life or his political career in jeopardy because of her.

"I'm not going to let anyone hurt you," Peyton said. "Whatever I have to do to protect you, I'll do it."

"It's not fair for you to risk your life because somebody has a grudge against me."

He squeezed her hand with more strength than either he or Tallie imagined he possessed. "Something happened with us last night. We can't pretend it didn't."

Tallie cut her eyes in Spence's direction, wondering what on earth he thought about Peyt's comment. "Nothing happened, except you got shot. Twice."

Peyton grinned. Tallie blushed. Spence laughed.

"What time is it?" Peyton asked.

Spence checked his watch. "Nearly five-thirty."

"God, I'm hungry," Peyton said. "Would you believe it? Wonder when they serve breakfast around here."

"Probably not before seven or eight," Spence said. "But if you're really hungry, I can run out and pick up some biscuits for you. For all of us. Are you hungry, Tallie?"

"What?" All she could think about was the way Peyt was holding her hand, so tightly, so possessively, as if he never intended to let her go.

"I want two steak biscuits and some coffee," Peyton said. "What do you want, sugar? Some cinnamon-raisin biscuits? I know you love cinnamon."

Tallie had no idea how Peyt knew she loved cinnamon. She'd never dreamed that he paid such close attention to her likes and dislikes. "That'll be fine." Tallie tried to pull away from Peyton, but he held fast. "I could go with Pattie and get breakfast."

"You stay here with me." Peyton tugged on her hand until she sat down on the bed beside him. "You'll probably have to sneak the food past the nurses. They'll tell you that I can't have any decent food yet."

"Leave it to me, big brother." Spence waved goodbye.

"I could use another kiss," Peyton said. "It's good medicine for me."

"What happened to you in that operating room?" Tallie asked. "I've never seen you like this."

"You saw me like this last night."

"Nothing's changed for us, has it? I mean, we're still bad news for each other, aren't we?" Tallie's heart raced at breakneck speed.

"Things *have* changed. I could have died. Those shots could have killed me."

With tears blurring her vision, Tallie stared at Peyton's somber face. Her unsteady fingers reached out, tracing the hard, chiseled planes of his cheekbones and jaw. "If anything had happened to you... Oh, Peyt, I can't help the way I feel about you."

"Come here, sugar." He urged her closer until his lips brushed hers. "Last night when you were in danger, my only thought was of saving you. Nothing mattered but you. Do you understand what I'm saying? Obviously, I can't help the way I feel about you, either."

"How...how do you feel about me?" She felt his heated breath caress her face. She wanted to kiss him.

"Damned if I know for sure." He laughed, his gaze filled with warm humor. "I care a hell of a lot more than I want to." When she tried to withdraw, he wouldn't allow it. "I think maybe we owe it to ourselves to find out if we can have a relationship that won't destroy us both."

"But you said we were nothing but trouble for each other." His mouth was so close. Oh, Lord, if he didn't kiss her soon, she was going to die.

"That's true, but regardless of that, we want each other. I thought I could just cut you out of my life, but, after last night, I know that's not possible. Not as long as you want me as much as I want you."

He kissed her then, and it was all that Tallie had longed for—hot, wet, deep and filled with passion.

Thirty minutes later, when Spence and Pattie walked into Peyton's room, they found Tallie sitting in a chair beside Peyt's bed, their hands still entwined while Peyton slept peacefully.

"Breakfast has arrived," Spence whispered as he and Pattie made their way into the room as quietly as possible.

"And the morning paper," Pattie added, laying the *Marshallton News* on the bedside table.

Peyton opened his eyes, a drug-induced grogginess in his expression. "How long have I been asleep?"

"About twenty minutes," Tallie told him.

He squeezed her hand. "How about a cup of coffee and a quick look at the paper?"

Pattie pushed the button that raised the head of Peyt's bed while Spence handed him a cup of coffee from the fast-food restaurant. Tallie gave him the morning paper.

Spence spread the contents of the two paper sacks containing various biscuits and coffee cups atop the portable meal tray at the foot of Peyton's bed.

"Eat it while it's hot," he said.

"I'll be damned!" Peyton bellowed, crushing the newspaper in his fist.

"What's wrong?" Tallie reached for the paper, but Peyton refused to release it.

"Some of your stocks go down?" Spence asked.

"Call Harrison Black at the *Marshallton News* and tell him that he's looking at a lawsuit." Peyton flung the newspaper on the floor. "He'd better get control of his reporters if he wants to keep that rag in business."

"What the hell did they print that's got you so riled?" Spence asked.

Tallie walked around to where Peyt had thrown the paper, bent over, picked it up and smoothed out the wrinkled pages. She scanned the headlines. Then she saw it. A picture of her, crying hysterically, clinging to Peyton's hand when the paramedics rushed him into the emergency room. Beside that photograph was one of Peyton leading Tallie out of the courtroom, his arm around her waist. The caption read: "Peyton Rand, shot under mysterious circumstances, is comforted by his client, lovely tow-truck driver Tallie Bishop. What's the real scoop on these two? Is Ms. Bishop a candidate for first lady of the state?"

Tallie pressed the newspaper to her breast. No wonder Peyton was outraged. What if the Memphis or Nashville papers picked up the story? This type of publicity would be detrimental to Peyt's political career.

"Tallie, sugar, don't get upset," Peyton said.

"Here, let me see that paper." Spence pulled the newspaper away from Tallie, took a look and then grunted. "So big deal. Maybe we should read the article before we jump to any conclusions and threaten Harrison with a lawsuit."

"You're right," Peyton said. "I just don't like the idea of the press implying things about Tallie. Take a look at the picture from the trial."

Spence unfolded the paper and looked at the photo at the bottom of the page. "You look very protective, big brother, with your arm around Tallie and such a fierce expression on your face."

"This is wrong." Tallie glanced around the room from Peyton to Spence to Pattie and back to Peyton again. "I can't let our involvement hurt your chances of running for governor."

"Don't get so upset about this, sugar." Peyton motioned for her to come to him. "Hey, I haven't decided if I want to get into politics."

Tallie stood her ground, refusing to go to Peyton. "Who are you kidding? All of us know that you've been building toward a political career for years now. Dammit, Peyt, the whole state of Tennessee is expecting you to announce your candidacy."

"Maybe I've changed my mind, but even if I haven't, that doesn't mean you and I—"

"There is no you and me!" Tallie ran from the room.

"Hell!" Peyton grumbled. "Spence, go get her. Bring her back in here. I'll be damned if I'll let her walk out on me now."

"Now?" Spence asked. "What's different about now?"

"Now that I've been shot. Now that I realize I'd die to protect Tallie Bishop. Now that I've admitted to myself that I'm more like the Senator than I ever wanted to be, but I'm not going to let my aspirations get in the way of my happiness."

Grinning, Spence rushed out into the hallway. Tallie stood with her back resting against the wall. She stared at him through tear-filled eyes. He placed his hand on her shoulder.

"Peyt wants you to come back inside. He wants to talk."

"I can't go back in there."

"You should. What he said to me made more sense than anything he's ever said." Spence nodded at his brother's closed hospital door. "He needs you, Tallie."

"How can you say that? I'm the last woman on earth he needs. People are already saying that we're having an affair. How do you think that looks?"

"You're both single. I don't see the harm in people speculating about your love life."

"Please go back in there and tell Peyt that I'm going to do him a big favor and get out of his life once and for all." Tallie shrugged off Spence's comforting hold. "Tell him he's been right all along. We're nothing but trouble for each other, and the best thing we can do to protect ourselves is to stay as far away from each other as we possibly can."

"Tallie, you don't mean what you're saying," Spence said. "You're overreacting to those pictures in the paper. Don't throw away any chance for happiness you and Peyt might have out of some noble sense of—"

"No!" Tallie covered her ears with her open palms. "I'm not listening."

Before Spence had a chance to reply, Tallie ran down the hall, wanting desperately to escape before she started listening to Peyt's brother, before she weakened and gave in to what her heart was telling her.

Peyton sat upright in the bed watching the door for Tallie's return. Instead, Spence walked in alone.

"Where is she?" Peyt asked.

"Gone," Spence said.

"Why did you let her leave? I told you to stop her."

"What did you want me to do, knock her out and drag her back in here?"

"Damn!" Peyt slammed his fists together, jerking out the IV tube attached to his left hand.

"I'll get the nurse," Pattie said. "See if you can calm him down."

"I don't want to be calmed down. I want Tallulah Bishop, and I want her now. She can't be allowed out there alone. Someone tried to kill her last night."

"I'll talk to Lowell." Spence nodded for his wife to leave; then he sat down in the chair beside his brother's bed. "Maybe Lowell can arrange some sort of protection for Tallie. But the best thing you can do for Tallie and yourself is take it easy, rest and recuperate. A couple of days in here and you can go to Tallie, tell her how you feel and take care of her."

"All right. All right." Peyton leaned back against the raised bed. "I want you to promise me that you'll talk to Tallie and get her to come to Marshallton and stay with you and Pattie until I get out of the hospital."

"I'll talk to her, but I don't think she'll change her mind. She told me to tell you that she's going to do you a big favor and get out of your life once and for all."

"Damn!"

"I thought that was what you wanted," Spence said. "Ever since I came home to Marshallton, all I've heard out of you about Tallie is how you wished you'd never gotten stuck baby-sitting her, how you wished—"

"Just shut up, will you? A man can change his mind, can't he?"

Tallie wiped her hands off on the orange grease rag, stuck it in her back pocket and leaned over the open hood of the '69 Pontiac Firebird she and Mike were restoring for a client.

During the four days since she'd run out of the hospital, leaving Peyton Rand and his political career behind her, she had thrown herself into her work. Spence and Pattie had stopped by three days ago and tried to persuade her to come home with them and stay until the authorities had found the man who'd shot Peyt. She had refused their offer.

Tallie wasn't foolish enough to be fearless. She was afraid. She knew full well that out there somewhere was a man who hated her so much, he wanted to see her dead. She kept Solomon with her all the time, and her shotgun was no longer filled with birdshot. She'd spent the last few nights with Sheila, with Mike staying over, too, sleeping on the sofa. She'd taken Richie Nolan's Whitey and her own Sheba along with her. Whitey and Sheila's son, Danny, had taken an instant liking to each other, so Tallie knew that when she went home, she'd be leaving Whitey behind.

Tallie didn't need help from the Rands. She had other friends.

An old rock tune played on the radio. A warm breeze wafted through the open garage door, picking up the strong scents of grease and gasoline that permeated the air inside the block structure.

"That looks like Sheriff Redman's car." Mike held a box-end wrench in his hand as he bent over the hood to tighten the bolts in the power-steering pump.

Tallie glanced out into the parking area where a late-model Chevrolet had stopped. Lowell Redman emerged from the vehicle, took off his hat and tossed it on the seat before closing the door.

"Afternoon, Tallie, Mike." Lowell patted Solomon on the head as he passed the Great Dane standing guard in front of a huge oscillating fan just inside the garage.

"Any word on the man who shot Rand?" Mike asked.

"Well, we've questioned Lobo Smothers. He has an alibi. His girlfriend swears he was with her all night. But we haven't found Cliff Nolan, yet. His friends tell us he's out hunting for Loretta and the kids."

"I hope he never finds them," Tallie said. "Come on back, Lowell. Would you care for a cola?"

"No, thanks." Lowell lifted his leg, bracing his foot on a discarded tire lying beside the Firebird. "We found the truck deserted on a back road about fifteen miles from your house."

"And?" Tallie wanted this nightmare to end, for her life to return to normal, for her to be able to stop feeling guilty about Peyton Rand's gunshot wounds.

"The truck was stolen. It belonged to some old pig farmer down in Mississippi." Lowell placed his hands on his hips, one hand lightly resting atop his holster. "The gun was in the truck, just lying there on the seat. We're running a check on it, but I figure it was stolen, too. Might even belong to the pig farmer."

"So you aren't any closer to finding the man who shot Peyton than you were four days ago." Tallie wiped the sweat from her forehead with the back of her hand.

"There's always the possibility that whoever shot Peyton didn't mean to kill anyone," Lowell said. "He might have intended scaring you, warning you to stay out of his life."

"Even if your theory is right, that doesn't change the fact that this man committed a crime. Even if I don't have anything to fear from him, he's still got to be captured and punished for what he did to Peyton." Tallie turned to Mike. "I'll walk Lowell out. I need to talk to him privately."

Mike nodded. Rounding the hood of the Pontiac, Tallie motioned for Lowell to follow her.

"What is it, Tallie?"

"I was just wondering if you'd heard anything from Peyt today."

Lowell stared at her when they walked out into the sunshine, his eyes narrowing to slits. "He's well enough to issue me orders left and right."

"That's good." Tallie tried to smile.

"He's getting out of the hospital today. Probably already out by now. I wouldn't doubt that Donna Fields drove him home." Lowell looked upward, scratched his throat and said, "Yeah, she was over there visiting when I stopped by this morning."

Tallie told herself that the fact that Donna Fields was playing nursemaid to Peyton shouldn't bother her. But it did. It bothered her a hell of a lot.

"Well, good," Tallie said. "She's just the thing he needs."

"Yeah, I suppose you're right about that." Lowell opened his car door. "You take care of yourself, Tallie. Stay out of trouble, but call me if you need me."

"Thanks."

Tallie watched the sheriff leave, all the while willing herself not to think about Peyton and how very close they'd come to being lovers the night he'd been shot. If only... No, she wasn't going to keep on daydreaming about something that wasn't meant to be.

She had made her decision four days ago when she'd left the hospital. She was not going to put Peyton's life or his future in jeopardy, and if she didn't end their relationship before it really began, then she was bound to wind up causing them both nothing but heartache. She figured they were better off apart, especially Peyton. He'd said himself that he wasn't in love with her, that he was only attracted to her—sexually.

Stop it! her mind screamed. For the past few nights, she hadn't been able to sleep for thinking about Peyton, remembering the feel of his lips on hers, his thrusting tongue mating with hers, his hands caressing her, his husky voice calling her *sugar*.

Just as Tallie turned to go back inside the garage, she heard another car pull into the parking lot and Mike call out to her.

"Looks like this is our day for visitors, but no customers."

Tallie glanced around just in time to see Peyton Rand easing himself out of his Jag. Knotting her hands into fists, she approached him, telling herself she was strong enough to face him, brave enough to do the right thing.

"Glad to see you're out of the hospital," she said.

"Are you? You have a strange way of showing concern, Tallie. No visits, not even a phone call."

"Spence and Pattie gave me an update on your condition when they stopped by to ask me to come stay a while with them. And Lowell told me only a few minutes ago that you were well enough to be released today."

"Why didn't you go stay with Spence and Pattie?"

"I don't need help from the Rands. Not anymore." Tallie stared down at the pavement beneath her feet.

"You need protection until the gunman is found," Peyton said. "You shouldn't be alone."

"I'm not alone. I've been staying with Sheila, and Mike's been sleeping over."

"Mike, huh? Is he in the bodyguard business now?"

"Yeah, I suppose he is. I understand Donna Fields has gone into nursing." Oh, hell's toenails, she hadn't meant to say that. How could she have just blurted out her jealousy that way? "I think Donna's just the right person to be in your life. You two really are perfect for each other, you know."

Peyton took a step forward; still looking downward, Tallie stepped back. Peyton reached out, grabbing her by the shoulders.

"Look at me, Tallie, and tell me what the hell's going on."

"Nothing's going on. Absolutely nothing." She didn't know if she could look directly at him and continue lying to him.

He tilted her chin. She shut her eyes. He pulled her closer.

"If you won't move into Marshallton with Pattie and Spence until the gunman is captured, then I'll just have to move out here to Crooked Oak with you."

"No, you can't do that!"

"Why not?"

"Are you out of your mind? Think about the publicity."

"To hell with the publicity."

Tallie jerked away from him, backing up as she stared at his sultry, sexy smile. What was the matter with him? He wasn't acting like the Peyton Rand she'd known most of her life.

"I think when they removed those bullets from your arm and side, they made a detour and operated on your brain." Tallie held up both hands in front of her to warn him off when he reached out for her again. "Get this straight, Peyt. I have set you free. I'm out of your life for good. No more calls for help. No more pleas to get me out of trouble. I'm a big girl now and I can take care of myself."

"Is that right?" Peyton backed her up against the outside garage wall. "Well, the way I see it, I saved your life the other night, and that gives me certain privileges."

"Just what privileges do you think it gives you, Rand?" Mike Hanley asked as he placed the wrench in a toolbox and wiped off his hands on his coveralls.

"Stay out of this, Hanley. This is between Tallie and me," Peyton said.

"Is that the way you want it, Tallie?" Mike walked outside, stopping a couple of feet away from Tallie and Peyton.

"Mike, why don't you go get us all a cold drink out of the machine? By the time you do that, Peyt and I should be finished with our conversation and he can take his cola with him when he leaves."

Frowning, Mike nodded agreement and went inside the office where the cola machine was located.

"If you won't stay with Pattie and Spence, and you don't want me moving in with you, then I see only one other alternative," Peyton said.

"Just what is that, pray tell?"

"I'll put in calls to Caleb and Hank and Jake, and tell them what's happened. I think your three brothers would be the best bodyguards anyone could ask for, don't you?"

"Don't you dare threaten me." Tallie shoved her index finger into Peyton's chest. "You will not call my brothers and interfere in their lives. Do you hear me?"

"Sugar, your life is in danger, and I'm not about to let anything happen to you." He covered her hand with his, trapping it against his chest.

"All of this concern is over sex, isn't it?" She knew what she said wasn't true, but she had to get Peyton out of her life, she had to convince him that if he was smart, he'd get away from her while he could.

"What are you talking about?" Peyton pulled her into his arms. "If you're asking whether or not I want to make love to you, then the answer is yes. But you already knew that. You found out just how much I want you the other night."

"Well, I suppose I've wanted you for a long time. I've always been curious what it would be like with you. Men are all different, you know, and I guess I just wondered if you'd be as good in bed as Mike—"

Peyton gripped her in his arms so tightly she cried out. His blue eyes turned to sapphire flame. "Don't try to convince me that you're sleeping with Hanley. I don't believe it."

"Believe what you want, Peyt. You always have. You really are just like your father, aren't you? Bulldozing over people to get your way, thinking you know what's best for everybody else." She knew only too well how much Peyt hated the comparisons between himself and Marshall Rand, how desperately Peyt tried not to emulate the Senator in spite of how much the two men resembled each other.

She hadn't expected the kiss, so when it came, she reacted instinctively, accepting Peyton's passion, responding ardently. She clung to him, the world around them blurring into hazy shades of unreality. Then she heard the sound of someone clearing his throat. It took her several moments to realize what was happening, what she had allowed to happen and was indeed encouraging to continue.

"Got grape sodas for all of us," Mike said.

Peyton released Tallie. She stepped back, away from him. Mike handed Peyton his cola, then placed one in Tallie's hand as he put his arm around her waist and pulled her up against him.

Peyton stared at the couple, then down at the grape soda in his hand. "Tallie tells me that you're keeping an eye on her."

"That's right. From now on, I'll take care of Tallie. She wants it that way, don't you, sweetheart?"

Tallie couldn't find her voice for a few moments, then she looked at Mike and smiled. "That's right, honey. I was trying to tell Peyton he's a free man, that now I've got you and I won't be bothering him to come and get me out of any more jams."

Peyton glared at Tallie. "Are you sure this is the way you want it?"

She knew he was giving her one last chance to change her mind. Since she'd been sixteen, she'd been in love with Peyton Rand, had dreamed of being his woman. Now, after all this time, he'd finally made the offer and she couldn't accept. For his sake. She loved him far too much to destroy his life, to drag his name through any more scandal, to be the cause of his political career's demise.

"Yes," she said. "This is the way I want it."

Peyton didn't say a word. He set the grape soda on a nearby window ledge, then gave her one last, hard look before he walked off, got in his Jag and drove away.

The minute the dark blue car disappeared, Tallie fell into Mike's open arms, tears dampening her cheeks.

"Why'd you do it, Tallie? You must love that guy an awful lot."

"Oh, Mike, I do. I love him more than life itself."

Six

Tallie tapped her foot to the beat of the country song the band played, an old Eddy Arnold tune she recognized because it had been one of her grandfather's favorites. Sheila giggled at something Susan Williams said, then downed the last drops of her beer. For at least the fifth time in the past hour, Tallie wondered what she and her two best friends were doing at the Pale Rider. She'd been here several times over the years, but this was Sheila's and Susan's first visit. Susan had refused anything alcoholic, and Sheila, on her second beer, was already a little light-headed. Her friends were as out of place in Marshallton's most popular night spot as a French courtesan would be in a Baptist Sunday school.

Tallie knew the only reason Sheila and Susan had agreed to this wild night on the town was in the hopes of dragging her out of the depression she'd been in the last month, ever since she had let Peyton Rand walk out of her life. Oh, she'd kept up the pretense that everything was normal, but those closest to her knew better. She wasn't sure she would have survived these last few weeks without Susan, Sheila and Mike, not to mention the never-failing love of Solomon and Sheba. People who'd never known the devotion of a faithful pet had missed one of life's sweetest joys.

"This is a very interesting place," Susan said, glancing around at the huge, smoky interior of the rowdy, let-the-good-times-roll honky-tonk.

"Reminds me of the inside of Uncle Joe's old barn." Sheila breathed deeply. "And it doesn't smell much better."

"Sweat and beer and cigarette smoke do combine to make a unique odor, don't they?" Susan circled her glass of cola with her hand, rubbing the edge with her thumb. "Wonder why people come to a place like this?"

"You mean why are *we* in a place like this?" Tallie smiled as she looked out on the dance floor where dozens of couples shuffled around in each other's arms.

"Some people get lonely," Sheila said. "They come here looking for escape, hoping they can find someone to hold them, to listen to them, to care about them, even if it's only for a few hours."

Tallie glanced over at Sheila, who was no longer giggling. Loneliness was a constant in Sheila's life. She'd been a widow for years, and wouldn't even consider dating. Her husband had been years older than she, and everyone had been surprised when the eighteen-year-old, plain and plump Sheila Hanley had married Claude Bishop's business partner, a widower in his late forties.

"I'm not sure I'd want to spend the rest of my life with the type of man you'd meet in this place." Susan lifted her glass to her lips, took a sip, returned it to the table and glanced around the room again, her nose slightly tilted in the air.

"Susan Williams, you're a snob," Tallie said. "Besides, you like animals better than you like men. You always have.

When we were in high school, you'd be out riding your horse or romping around in the fields with one of your dogs while the other girls were learning the facts of life in the back seats of their boyfriends' cars."

"Look who's talking." Susan pointed at Tallie. "You were too busy mooning over Peyton Rand to date other guys in high school."

Tallie's smile vanished. She didn't want to think about Peyt, didn't want to remember how many years of her life she'd spent waiting for him to love her.

"Now you've gone and done it," Sheila said. "That's the one name we weren't supposed to mention tonight."

"It's all right," Tallie said. "Not mentioning his name won't keep me from thinking about him, about what a complete fool I am."

"You know, I feel like dancing," Sheila said. "I suppose it's out of the question for me to ask one of you to dance. People would probably get the wrong idea. Just think what Maude Simmons would write in her 'Around and About Crooked Oak' column in the *Marshallton News*."

The three women looked at one another, then burst into laughter. The laughter helped release the tension that had built up inside Tallie. Thank God for good friends, she thought.

"Listen to that song, would you? It's enough to make you cry." Susan's tone was dead serious, but she could not refrain from giggling.

Suddenly, all three friends were laughing again, the uncontrollable, giddy laughter that brings on tears and side cramps.

Tallie threw up her hands in a gesture of submission, pleading with her friends to stop so that she could end her own unrestrained laughter. "We've got to stop this or they'll throw us out of here."

"You've got to be kidding." Sheila swung out her arm, indicating to her friends that they should look around. "Who could hear us with all that noise?"

Susan stared at the bar area on the other side of the room. "Oh, no. What's he doing here?"

"Who is it?" Sheila asked.

Tallie glanced in the direction of Susan's riveted stare. "Damn! It's Eric Miller. If he sees me, I'll have the devil's own time getting rid of him."

"We could leave right now," Sheila suggested.

"We might not want to do that," Susan said.

"Why?" Tallie noticed that Susan's gaze was no longer fixed on the bar, but on the entrance to the Pale Rider.

"Peyton Rand!" Tallie couldn't believe her eyes.

"If we leave now, we'll have to walk right past him." Susan shook her head. "This night is turning out to be a lot more interesting than I ever thought it would."

"Surely there's a back way out." Sheila surveyed the room. "We could go hide in the ladies' room."

"I'm not going anywhere," Tallie said. "The Pale Rider has a bouncer or two. If Eric bothers me, I'll just have him thrown out on his ear."

"What about Peyton Rand?" Susan asked.

"I'm not sure why he's here, but believe me, he isn't going to bother me."

"Yeah, sure." Susan shook her head.

"Uh-huh." Grunting, Sheila rolled her eyes upward.

Peyton hadn't been inside the Pale Rider for years. It wasn't his usual kind of night spot. He preferred the more sophisticated places in Memphis. But he'd agreed to meet Lowell Redman here for a few beers. Lowell had told him that he liked to hit a few of the local night spots when he went off duty to keep an unofficial eye on things.

Peyton made his way across the room, past the dance floor and row after row of small tables filled with beer-drinking rednecks. These local good-old-boys were his constituency, the people who could help elect him. Like his father before him, he could lay claim to country roots, could profess a kinship with the county's common people, could mix and mingle, hunt and fish, out-drink, out-cuss, out-fight any man in the place. And tomorrow night he could attend a thousand-dollar-a-plate charity function with the elite of Tennessee society and claim fellowship with them, lay claim to similar wealth and breeding, could mix and mingle, discuss stocks and bonds, drink expensive liquor and outmaneuver any smart businessman in the place.

Peyton Rand, the people's choice. A man at home anywhere. A born politician. Like his father before him.

Peyton shuddered at the thought, but he'd long ago accepted the fact that he was his father's son in many ways. He knew his only hope of not destroying himself and others the way his father had done was to keep a check on himself, on the powerful traits he had inherited.

Peyton found an empty table several yards back from the dance floor. The waitress took his order for a beer. He would have ordered Scotch, but he doubted the liquor served at the Pale Rider could even begin to compare with what he was used to drinking. He was used to the best, and it wasn't in his nature to accept less.

He was a little early, but traffic had been light on the drive from Jackson. He didn't mind waiting a while for Lowell. The distractions of the band, the noisy chatter and the attractive waitresses just might take his mind off the major problem in his life. Tallulah Bankhead Bishop.

He hadn't seen her for a month, not since he'd left her in Mike Hanley's arms. When he'd driven away that day, he'd been consumed with anger and jealousy, but within an hour he'd calmed down enough to come to his senses and realize just what had happened. Tallie had given the performance of her life. She'd done what she thought was best for him. For him, damn her, not for herself.

No doubt Tallie had figured out that if the two of them pursued an affair, it could well be the end of any political aspirations he might have. He wasn't so sure anymore about what a relationship with Tallie would mean to his future plans. In the month he'd been separated from Tallie—the longest period in their acquaintance they'd gone without seeing each other—Peyton had come to a few heartfelt conclusions. By denying his baser feelings for Tallie, he hadn't been protecting her, but himself. He'd been afraid of a relationship with a woman like Tallie. He'd instinctively known that he could not have an affair with her, become emotionally and physically involved with her without allowing her to influence him, indeed to change him.

Tallie was the most honest woman he'd ever known. No pretensions. Nothing false. A basic what-you-see-is-what-you-get kind of person. She didn't play games, didn't even try to learn the rules of polite society. Tallie loved life, loved people, loved animals. She opened herself up to every experience, reached out and brought the world into her arms. When someone else ached with pain, Tallie cried. When someone was in need, Tallie tried to fill that need.

Peyton had spent the past eight years denying his desire for Tallie, and now that he'd finally admitted to her how much he wanted her, she had rejected him—in order to protect him. What if he didn't want protection? What if he was willing to risk everything for the chance to become Tallie's lover?

And what the hell difference did it make now? Tallie was out of his life for good. Maybe he was lucky. Maybe she really had spared them both a lot of unnecessary pain.

Accepting the cold beer the waitress offered him, Peyton leaned back in the wooden chair, spreading his long legs out in front of him and crossing them at the ankles. He closed his eyes for a couple of seconds as he listened to the band's rendition of George Strait's hit, "You're Something Special to Me.'' Peyton knew and liked country music, although he usually preferred jazz or even certain classical works. This particular tune seemed entirely appropriate at the moment, considering his thoughts about Tallie Bishop. He supposed he'd always thought of Tallie as an angel, if somewhat tarnished around the edges, and he knew only too well how special she was, not only to him, but to everyone who knew her.

But if Tallie hadn't put a stop to their sexual relationship before it ever started, would he have had the guts to profess his feelings for her to the world?

Enough of this melodramatic brooding! Opening his eyes, Peyton glanced around the dim, smoke-filled room, wishing that he'd taken his time getting here, wishing that Lowell would hurry. The last thing he needed was time on his hands to think about Tallie.

Dammit all, was he hallucinating? he wondered. Had he thought about the woman so much, he was seeing her even when she wasn't there?

Peyton glanced away from the table behind him where three women sat staring at him. Drawing in a deep breath, he turned slightly and took a second look. Hell! Sheila Vance, Susan Williams and Tallie Bishop. He hadn't been seeing things. What were they doing here?

His gaze locked with Tallie's. Her face looked pale, her eyes misty. Was she on the verge of tears? He wanted to reach out and touch her, to draw her into his arms and hold her close. Despite the peace and calm he'd enjoyed in his life for the last few weeks, the reality of how much he'd missed Tallie hit him full force.

He never took his eyes off Tallie while he gulped down a swig of beer, scooted back his chair and stood. He noticed the way she sat up straighter, the way her body tensed with anticipation when she saw him getting up and walking toward her.

She looked up at him when he stopped beside her table. Damn, what pure innocence shone in those pale brown eyes, such undisguised longing, such sweet honesty.

"How are you, Tallie?" he asked.

"I'm fine, Peyt. And you?" He looked wonderful, she thought, more wonderful than in her dreams.

"I'm okay. Keeping busy at work." I've missed you, sugar, missed you so bad I've ached day and night with wanting to see you, to hear your voice, to touch you.

"How's Pattie and Spence? And Donna?"

"My brother and his wife were well the last time I talked to them. And I suppose Donna's okay, too. I haven't seen her in a while. How's Mike?"

"Mike's fine." Mike is such a dear, sweet man, and I wish I were in love with him instead of you. I wish that every time I looked at him I melted into a puddle at his feet, the way I do with you.

"Mike had to work tonight," Sheila said. "That's the reason he's not with Tallie."

Peyton turned his attention momentarily to the other two women at the table. "Good evening, ladies. Y'all having fun tonight?"

"Oh, yes," Susan said. "We're having a ball."

"Would you two mind if I took Tallie away for a few minutes?" Peyton held out his hand to Tallie.

"She can't go anywhere right now." Staring at Tallie, Susan shook her head in a negative gesture.

Sheila grabbed Tallie's hand. "Mike's the jealous type, you know."

"All I want is a dance." Lifting Tallie's hand into his, Peyton urged her to stand.

Making no protest, she simply stood and followed him out onto the dance floor. An old George Jones tune, "The Grand Tour," was the band singer's choice for the next number. The beat was slow, the lyrics heartbreaking, the rhythm body-hugging. The sweet, hard blending of guitar, piano and drums created the background for the singer's soft, soulful rendition of lost love and pure country passion and pain.

Peyton slipped his arms around Tallie, drawing her into his embrace. She knew this was a mistake, knew she'd live to regret it, but she simply didn't have the strength to resist one more chance to be in Peyton's arms.

He couldn't remember a time when a woman had felt so right in his arms, when he'd known in his heart that she belonged with him. But how was he going to convince Tallie?

He buried his chin in her hair, the top of her head resting against his chest. "You smell so good, sugar. Like sunshine and roses."

"Why are you here, Peyt? Why are you doing this to me?" Didn't he know how difficult it had been for her to send him away, to give up the one chance they might have had to be together?

"I didn't follow you here or anything like that. I'm meeting Lowell for a few drinks." Peyton lowered his hand from her waist to the hollow just above her hips. "He's been keeping me posted on the investigation into the shooting, and letting me know how you've been getting along."

"I told you I've been just fine." She ran her hand across his shoulder and down his arm. "No one's taken any more shots at me. I think Lowell's right about his theory that someone, maybe Cliff Nolan or Lobo Smothers, just wanted to scare me."

"I hope Lowell's right. I wouldn't want anything happening to you." He kissed her tenderly on the forehead. "I worry about you."

"Old habits die hard, huh?" She tried to make the comment sound like a joke, but knew she'd failed when Peyton tightened his hold on her, drawing her closer against his aroused body.

She cried out silently, startled by the feel of Peyton's hard body, so obviously in need of hers.

"You aren't having an affair with Mike Hanley, are you?"

"No, of course I'm not."

"I'm not having an affair with Donna Fields."

"I know." She dared to look up at him then, and realized that if she didn't escape right now, she would be lost—they'd both be lost.

When she tried to pull away from him, he held her close. "Peyt, don't do this. We'll both regret it."

"Do you want me to let you go?"

"Yes." Tears gathered in her eyes, one lone drop falling onto her cheek. "Please."

He released her immediately, the music continuing, the other couples dancing on to the sweet, sad melody. Tallie walked away. Watching her, Peyton stood alone on the dance floor.

Her vision obscured by the veil of tears covering her eyes, Tallie accidently bumped into someone as she exited the dance floor.

"Excuse me." Not even glancing at the man, she shifted her body to move around him.

He grabbed her by the shoulders. "Where are you going in such a hurry, sexy gal?"

At the sound of his voice, Tallie blinked away her tears as she jerked her head upward to face Eric Miller's smirk. "Leave me alone." She tried to pull away from him.

"Aw, now, don't be like that." Eric slipped his arm around her waist, dragging her up against him. "Come on and dance with me. I promise you won't run away from me the way you ran away from pretty boy."

"I don't want to dance with you, Eric. You're drunk." Exerting all her strength, Tallie tried to escape from Eric's tenacious embrace.

"Ah, sexy gal, I like the way you wiggle around. You're getting me all hot and bothered." He cupped her buttocks in his hands.

"Get your hands off me!" Tallie screamed, taking advantage of the moment to give Eric a shove.

The sudden push catching Eric off guard, he staggered backward, releasing Tallie. She turned, intending to rush away as quickly as she could, but before she moved two feet, Eric caught her by the shoulder.

"I ain't through with you, sexy gal. Not by a long shot."

"I think you are." Peyton stood directly behind Tallie, his gaze dead center on Eric's sweaty face.

Eric laughed, the sound a blend of cockiness and inebriation. "You don't do my thinking for me, Rand."

"This time, I do. And any time when Tallie's involved." Peyton grabbed Eric's meaty hand where it clutched Tallie's shoulder. "I warned you what would happen if you ever touched Tallie again."

"I'm scared to death." Chuckling, Eric flung Peyton's hand away.

"Please, Peyt, think about what you're doing," Tallie said. "If you get in a fight with Eric, think what the newspapers will print."

"Yeah, Mr. Fancy Pants, you'd better think of your reputation. Wouldn't want your old man turning over in his grave, would you?"

"Move away from him," Peyton ordered Tallie.

Tallie obeyed. But instead of removing herself from between the two men, she planted herself squarely in front of Peyton, only inches separating their bodies.

"They've got bouncers in this place," Tallie said. "Let them handle this."

"Aw, come on, sexy gal, let Senator Rand's little boy come out and play with me."

"Don't let him goad you into a fight." Tallie tugged on Peyton's sleeve. When he gazed down at her, she saw something in his face that she didn't recognize at first. The controlled, debonair, modern man had vanished, replaced by an angry, savage, fierce warrior. "Peyton?"

Lifting Tallie off her feet, Peyton set her aside. She couldn't move, couldn't speak, could barely think. Oh, God, Peyton and Eric were going to fight. Over her. She had to stop this madness.

Eric crouched slightly, his big body swaying, preparing for an attack. "I'm ready anytime you are, Rand."

"I don't want to fight," Peyton said, standing straight and tall, only the hard, cold glint in his eyes revealing any sign of emotion. "But I will not allow you to continue harassing Tallie. Do I make myself clear?"

Eric grinned, righted himself, pulled back his arm and threw the first punch, aiming it directly at Peyton's stomach. Acting quickly, Peyton avoided the hit. Filled with hot fury, Eric reared back, his eyes focusing on his opponent.

"Think you're so smart, don't you?" Eric stomped the wooden floor, snorted, then spit on a spot between his spread feet. "I'm going to mop the floor with you, pretty boy."

Eric lunged at Peyton, who again outmaneuvered the heavier man, but when Eric tried again, he landed a blow to Peyton's shoulder. Peyton thrust out his fist, striking Eric on the jaw. Eric staggered back only a fraction, then swung out again.

Making their way through the crowd of onlookers, Sheila and Susan hurried to Tallie's side.

"What happened?" Sheila asked.

"Eric grabbed me and tried to force me to dance," Tallie said. "Peyton demanded that Eric leave me alone."

"I can't watch this," Susan said. "It's so ridiculous for two grown men to fight."

"Please, go find the bouncers." Tallie scanned the crowd, searching for help. "I don't understand why they haven't stopped this."

"I heard someone say that the bouncers were handling another fight by taking the guys out to the parking lot," Sheila said.

Peyton and Eric, well-matched in height and muscle, landed several more blows before Eric, heavier and half-drunk, showed signs of weakening. Eric sported a bruised jaw and a blackening eye while Peyton's only battle scar was a bleeding lip.

The moment Tallie saw blood trickling from the side of Peyton's mouth, she cried out, momentarily distracting him from the task at hand. Taking advantage of the situation, Eric struck, landing a resounding blow to Peyton's mid-section, knocking the breath out of him and toppling him to the floor.

While Peyton struggled to regain his breath, Tallie flung herself at Eric, her small, round fist moving upward, making contact with Eric's nose. She heard the crunching sound and saw the spurts of bright red blood before she realized what she'd done. Eric bellowed like a wounded bull, staggered back into a nearby table, all the while covering his nose with his hand as blood poured down over his mouth and chin, dripping onto his shirt.

"Oh, hell's toenails," Tallie said.

Eric moaned in pain, then hollered, "You broke my nose, damn you!"

Peyton rose to his feet, preparing to continue his defense of Tallie when he realized that she'd done a fairly good job of protecting him. Seeing the three muscle-heavy bouncers dispersing the crowd as they made their way toward the fight scene, Peyton slipped his arm around Tallie, drawing her back and away from Eric Miller.

"All right, folks," the oldest of the three bouncers, probably no more than twenty-three, said. "The show's over. Go on back to your tables."

The band had never stopped playing the whole time Peyton and Eric had been fighting, but the crowd's cheers and taunts had drowned out the music. Now, Tallie could hear the squeal of a guitar and the swish of a brush across a drum. An aching pain encompassed her hand. Staring down at the instrument of Eric's downfall, Tallie groaned when she noticed the swelling and beginnings of discoloration across her knuckles.

"Somebody want to tell us what happened here?" the blond, mustached bouncer asked.

"She broke my damned nose," Eric said, pointing at Tallie. "All I did was ask her to dance, and she broke my nose."

"This man was drunk and harassing the lady," Peyton told the bouncers. "This isn't the first incident. I'd warned Mr. Miller to stay away from her before."

"So you two were fighting over who was going to dance with this woman, huh?" the second bouncer, all of maybe twenty-one years old, asked.

"No, we were *not* fighting over who was going to dance with the lady." Peyton's patience was wearing thin. "Unless the laws were changed without someone's informing me, I believe a man is well within his rights to defend himself."

"Eric hit Peyt first." Slipping out of Peyton's hold around her waist, Tallie marched over to the oldest bouncer, the one she assumed was in charge. "This whole thing is Eric Miller's fault. The man can't take no for an answer."

"Are you Peyton Rand?" the blond bouncer asked. "The big Jackson lawyer who's fixing to run for governor?"

"Oh, no," Tallie moaned. That's all they needed! If this man recognized Peyton, then there was a good chance word would be all over Marshallton by morning. Good grief! There was no telling how many people at the Pale Rider knew who Peyton was.

"He most certainly is." Lowell Redman, his sheriff's badge gleaming brightly even in the smoky room, put his hand on the blond bouncer's shoulder. "What seems to be the problem, Tip?"

"A routine fistfight," Tip said. "Apparently, these two men had a slight disagreement over this wo—" he glanced at Peyton "—this lady."

"Yeah, and she broke my nose," Eric said. "What are you going to do about that?"

"I'm going to let you spend the night in jail," Lowell said. "After my deputies take you by the emergency room to have your nose checked."

"Hey, what about Rand? Ain't he going to jail?" Eric, blood still dripping slowly onto his shirt, nodded toward Peyton.

"No, Mr. Rand is going to take Ms. Bishop home." Lowell motioned to the two younger bouncers. "Take Mr. Miller to the manager's office to wait for my deputies."

"This ain't fair," Eric complained as the two bouncers led him away.

"Any problems on your part, Tip?" Lowell asked. "If not, then I think you've detained Mr. Rand long enough."

"We're sure sorry about this, Mr. Rand," Tip said, then turned to Tallie. "Are you all right, ma'am?"

"I'm fine." She wasn't fine. Her hand hurt like blue blazes, her head throbbed unmercifully and she was worried sick about this latest Tallie-got-Peyton-in-the-news incident. Word of this was bound to get out.

"First time I ever saw somebody as little as you down a guy that size." Tip chuckled, but when no one else laughed, he said his goodbyes and followed his assistants.

"Looks like I got here a little too late for the sideshow," Lowell said.

Peyton grinned. "You got here just in time to save me from a real hassle with those boys. They weren't in any mood to listen to my explanation."

"I suppose our having a drink would seem a little anti-climactic at this point, wouldn't it?" Lowell glanced over at Tallie. "I don't think you're doing so good. You look as white as a sheet."

"No...I...I'm okay. Really. Just—"

Sheila and Susan hovered around Tallie, Susan lifting Tallie's injured fist.

"Look at your hand. It's swollen and red and—"

"Hush!" Tallie cut her eyes in Peyton's direction.

"Get her some ice," he told Susan. "Go tell the bartender you need some ice wrapped up in a towel."

"No, please," Tallie said. "I just want to get out of here. I want to go home."

"Come on, we'll take you." Sheila nodded toward the exit.

"Have you forgotten that the three of us came in separate cars?" Tallie asked. "Besides, I'm perfectly capable of driving myself home."

"I'll take you," Peyton said. "We'll get someone to pick up your car."

"I'm going home now," Tallie told them. "No ice pack for my hand, no friends trying to figure out who's taking me home. Like I said, I just want to get out of here."

With all eyes on Tallie, no one said a word. Sheila and Susan nodded. Lowell shook his head. Peyton turned and walked away.

Susan handed Tallie her purse. "Are you sure you want to go home alone?"

"I'm sure." Tallie gave Sheila a hug. "Why do these things happen to me? Why can't I stay out of trouble?"

"What happened tonight wasn't your fault," Susan said.

"Susan's right." Lowell smiled at Susan, his blue eyes brightening when he looked at her. "Eric Miller is trouble for everybody, not just you. Sooner or later, he's going to wind up in prison."

"Look, everybody, the night's still young." Tallie hung her small black purse over her shoulder. "There's no need for y'all to leave. Stay here and entertain our sheriff." She turned to Lowell. "When's the last time you spent the evening with two beautiful women?"

Lowell's grin reminded Tallie of a little boy's. There was a childlike innocence to the way he smiled, the way a pale pink blush crept into his cheeks, in the adoring way he looked at Susan.

"Can't say I've ever had the pleasure." Lowell's smile widened.

Tallie gave Susan a nudge forward. "Ask Susan to dance, and Sheila will go back to the table and order a round of drinks for y'all."

With a few hesitant steps, Lowell stood directly in front of Susan. "Would you like to dance?"

Susan glanced over at Tallie, who smiled and nodded. "I'd like that, Sheriff Redman."

Lowell escorted Susan onto the dance floor. Sheila patted Tallie on the back. "Good job there, Ms. Cupid. Lowell's had an oversize crush on Susan for quite some time."

"She needs a good man in her life."

"I agree," Sheila said. "But there's just one problem with Lowell and Susan dancing."

"What's that?"

"Lowell forgot to make a call for his deputies to pick up Eric Miller."

Tallie laughed. "He'll remember in a few minutes. Besides, it won't hurt those overgrown little boys the management hired as bouncers to baby-sit Eric for a while."

"Tallie, you really should take care of your hand."

"I will as soon as I get home. You go on and order those drinks, and play chaperon."

The night air hit Tallie in the face the moment she stepped outside the Pale Rider. Pleasantly warm and refreshing, with a hint of rain. Taking in a deep breath, Tal-

lie rummaged in her purse for her keys. Her right hand hurt
something awful, so much that tears of pain glazed her
eyes. Using her left hand, she inserted the key into the lock
of her 1980 black Camaro. The car had been Caleb's pride
and joy. When he'd wrecked it one spring night before he
left for college, he'd tossed Tallie the keys and told her if
she repaired it, it was hers. She spent several years restoring it. Now it was *her* pride and joy.

Slipping inside, Tallie rested her head on the steering
wheel. Her good sense told her that it wasn't her fault Eric
Miller wouldn't leave her alone, that he'd created a scene
and Peyton had stepped into the middle of the situation.
But her emotions nagged her, reminding her that trouble
seemed to follow her wherever she went. No, that wasn't
right, she realized. Trouble followed her whenever there was
the possibility that Peyton Rand would be around to bail
her out of the jam.

Was it really her fault or was fate playing some sort of
cruel joke on her? The last thing she wanted was to create
any more problems for Peyton, to see his name linked with
hers in the newspapers.

Tap. Tap, tap, tap. Jerking her head around, Tallie faced
the tapping noise. Peyton stood on the opposite side of her
car, pecking on the window. She leaned over and unlocked
the door. He slid inside.

"Here, let me see your hand." He lifted her hand in his.
"Mmm-mmm. Looks rough, sugar. You really let him have
it, didn't you?"

"What are you doing out here, Peyt? I thought I told
you—"

"Like you said, old habits die hard. I guess I'm used to
taking care of you." He reached inside his pocket, pulled
out a small white towel and held it down on top of her
bruised hand.

She drew back her hand. "That's cold!"

"It's a makeshift ice pack."

"Peyt, what am I going to do with you?"

"I think that's my usual line, isn't it?"

When she saw the grin on his face, part of her wanted to slap him, another part wanted to break down and really cry, yet another part wanted to kiss him and kiss him and never stop kissing him.

"Sooner or later you're going to have to take out a restraining order against Miller." Peyton looked into her eyes, those pale brown eyes that spoke louder than any words ever could.

"You're probably right. It's just that I don't think Eric is a real danger to me. He's just got this . . . this thing for me."

"He's big and strong and determined. And he's a drunk. That combination makes him dangerous." Peyton ran the tip of his thumb over Tallie's wrist just above where he held the ice pack to her bruised knuckles. "You're out alone tonight, Tallie. No shotgun. No Solomon. You're not taking very good care of yourself."

"It's been a month since the shooting at my house. Not a single, solitary soul has bothered me. And what happened in there tonight with Eric happened in front of dozens of people. If you hadn't interfered, the bouncers would have taken care of things."

"I couldn't stand by and let Miller paw you." Peyton leaned over, across the console, until his breath fanned the curls around Tallie's face. "You didn't want him to touch you, and God knows, I didn't want him to touch you."

"Peyt, this is crazy, and we both know it."

"What's crazy?" he asked innocently. "That I brought you an ice pack for your injured hand? That I care what happens to you? That I've been going out of my mind for weeks now, wondering how you're doing, trying to think of any excuse to call you or come see you?"

"I can't believe this is happening." Tallie pulled back, jerking her hand away, letting the ice pack fall on the console. "I've spent the last eight years chasing you, and you've spent the last eight years running. I've used every little problem I've ever had to draw you into my life, and you've fussed and fumed about wanting nothing more than to get rid of me."

Peyton retrieved the ice pack, took Tallie's hand back in his and laid the towel atop her knuckles. "So, what's your point?"

"What's my point?" Shrugging, Tallie huffed. "The point is that we agreed you and I don't have a future. We're wrong for each other. Bad for each other. I want marriage and babies and a white picket fence. I'm a simple girl, an old-fashioned girl. I couldn't change. I couldn't stop being myself." Pausing, she stared at Peyton, waiting to see if he would say something.

"And?"

"And you're a complicated man with a complex, sophisticated life-style who has finally admitted to himself that he's attracted to me. Right?"

"Right." Peyton nodded affirmatively.

"But you want an affair." Tallie swallowed. "You want us to have sex, to work me out of your system."

"You make me sound heartless, sugar, as if I don't care about you." Peyton cradled her cheek in his hand, running his thumb across her bottom lip.

"We can't have an affair, Peyt. It would ruin your chances of running for governor, and it would break my heart."

Sharp pangs of regret, remorse and guilt assaulted Peyton. All these years, he had told himself that he was protecting Tallie by keeping their relationship nonsexual. Hell, he'd been fooling himself. He'd done it as much to protect himself as her. He'd always thought of himself first—what was best for him. Just like his father. Exactly like the great Senator Marshall Rand.

Even tonight, he hadn't considered Tallie's feelings as much as his own. She was right. He was the one who'd changed the rules in the middle of the game because he'd gotten sick and tired of the old rules. The night he'd been shot, he'd had every intention of making love to Tallie, knowing full well that she wasn't the kind of woman who'd be happy just having an affair.

Taking her left hand, Peyton put it on top of the towel; then he eased back in the seat. "You must think I'm a real bastard."

"I think you're wonderful," she said, not looking directly at him, but at a safety light in the parking lot glowing brightly over his shoulder. "I've always thought you were wonderful."

"How can you say that after the way I've treated you?"

"You're confused right now, that's all. You've come to a crossroads in your life and you're afraid you'll make the wrong decision. I think I'm a part of that confusion. If I were anybody besides the Bishop boys' little sister, the girl who's had a crush on you since she was sixteen, you'd have already carried me off to bed, and we both know it."

"Damn, have I been that obvious?" Peyton thought he'd hidden his true feelings for her quite well over the years; obviously he hadn't.

"I just figured it out recently," she admitted. "You want me, but you know I don't fit in your life. You don't fit into my life, either." She laughed, the sound mixed with tears. "If we have an affair, the newspapers will have a field day. And we can't get married. You don't love me, and people wouldn't vote for a man whose wife—"

Peyton covered her lips with his index finger. "Ah, Tallie, do you know what I fear the most in this life? I'm afraid of turning out just like my father. Of becoming a cold, heartless, uncaring bastard who steamrolls his way over everyone, who doesn't care what other people think or feel or need. I'm already so much his son. Spence hated me for years because he thought I was just a carbon copy of the old man."

"You're not your father." Tallie dumped the ice pack onto the floorboard, then reached out to take Peyton's face in both hands. "You may look like him, talk like him, smoke those damned cigars and charm the birds from the trees the way he did, but you're your own man."

"Do you know I contemplated asking Donna Fields to marry me because I knew she'd make the perfect wife for a politician. I don't love her, and she doesn't love me. That's just the sort of thing my father would have done. As a matter of fact, I doubt he loved my mother, just her family's money and connections."

"Stop doing this to yourself." Tallie caressed his face, loving every sharp, hard angle and plane of male perfection. "You're strong and brave and smart and caring. You'll make a wonderful governor. The best this state has ever had."

"You're just saying those things because you—"

"Because I love you. Yeah, I know. So if a great girl like me loves you, then that must mean you're a pretty great guy yourself."

"Tallie..."

She kissed him, her lips warm and soft and inviting. He returned the kiss as he reached out, gripping the back of her head in his hand, drawing her closer. But he ended the kiss before it got out of hand, before he lost control.

"I'm not going to break your heart, little heathen. I'm going to get out of your life before I do any more damage to it." Peyton opened the car door, stepped outside, then bent over, leaning into the passenger's side. "Promise me you'll take care of yourself."

"Peyt?"

"Goodbye, Tallulah Bishop. I'm going to miss you." He slammed the door and walked away.

Tallie sat there for endless minutes, the pain in her hand numbed by the agony in her heart. It was really over this time. No doubt about it. She'd seen the last of Peyton Rand.

Seven

Spence handed his brother a sandwich off the tray of edible delights Pattie had prepared earlier in the day, before she'd left for her Saturday shopping spree with their daughter, Allie. Peyton accepted the food, bit into the ham and cheese, then laid it down on the napkin beside his beer can on the end table. His cigar, the tip an inch of fragile ash, rested in a ceramic tray. He tried to focus his attention on the television set where his favorite team's game was in progress. But while he watched Caleb Bishop, the team's star pitcher, all he could think about was Caleb's baby sister—the woman he wanted desperately, the woman he'd cut out of his life forever.

"Who'd ever thought Caleb would be a pro making millions? I remember when he was just a skinny kid who was disappointed because he hadn't bagged a deer the way Jake and Hank had done." Spence delved his hand into the bowl of party mix, popped a handful into his mouth and munched loudly.

"Yeah, well, Caleb was always an athlete, not a hunter. If he'd spent as much time hunting as he did playing ball, he'd have gotten his buck. Probably more than one."

"When's the last time you saw Caleb?" Spence asked.

"I guess it's been two or three years." Peyton picked up his beer, downed the last drops, then crushed the can. "I drove to Atlanta for one of the games, and Caleb took me out on the town."

"When's the last time he's been back to Crooked Oak?"

"He's only been back once or twice since he left for college. He came back for Claude's funeral. I know he calls Tallie pretty often, and he flies her out to see him a few times a year."

Spence leaned back on the big leather sofa beside Peyton. "Once the Bishop boys left Crooked Oak, they left for good, didn't they?"

"Yeah, it seems that way," Peyton said. "But look at you, little brother. When you left Marshallton, you swore you'd never come back, and now here you are one of the town's leading citizens. Who knows, one of these days all three Bishop boys may return to their roots."

"Well, if they have as good a reason to return as I did, then they'll—" The jarring ring of the telephone interrupted Spence midsentence. Reaching over to the end table on his side of the sofa, he picked up the portable phone. "Hello. Yeah, well, he just happens to be here watching the game with me. Sure, hold on." Spence turned to Peyton. "Sheila Vance."

Spence handed Peyton the phone. "Sheila? Peyton Rand here. Is something wrong? Is Tallie all right?"

"She was fine when she and Susan left about thirty minutes ago," Sheila said. "I've been debating about what to do. I tried to talk them out of it, but they wouldn't listen."

"What did you try to talk them out of doing, Sheila? Where have they gone?"

"Susan received an anonymous phone call from someone saying that Lobo Smothers was going to be setting some new traps in Kingsley Woods today."

"Hell!" Peyton knew without asking another question precisely where Tallie and Susan had gone and what deep trouble the two women would be in if they actually did run across Lobo Smothers.

"Tallie took her camera. She and Susan are determined to get pictures of Lobo setting the traps."

"Did Tallie take Solomon? Did she take a gun?" Surely she hadn't gone off after Lobo without some form of protection.

"Solomon was in the car with them, and I think she took her...shotgun." Sheila's voice broke as she gulped back a sob. "I tried to contact Mike, but he's on the scene of a bad wreck out on Old Grady Road. I didn't know what to do, Mr. Rand. But the more I thought about it, the more worried I got. Anything could happen to them out there in the woods with a man like Lobo Smothers."

"Don't worry, Sheila," Peyton said. "I'll take care of everything."

When he returned the receiver to its cradle, Peyton slammed his fist into the fat back cushion of the sofa. "Damn that woman! She's going to get herself killed."

"What's Tallie done now?" Spence asked.

"Gone off to Kingsley Woods to try to catch Lobo Smothers setting illegal traps. And she's taken Susan Williams with her."

"I suppose you're going to drive down to Crooked Oak and—"

"I'm calling Lowell Redman and have him meet me at the old campsite near the creek." Peyton grabbed the phone, hammering out the numbers with brutal force. If Lobo Smothers harmed one hair on Tallie's head, he'd kill the S.O.B. And if Peyton got to Tallie first, he was going to... What? Shake some sense into her? Although both alternatives soothed his raging senses, a third alternative appealed to him even more—an alternative that included keeping Tallie Bishop in bed for at least twenty-four hours.

Kingsley Woods covered several hundred acres of land between the small town of Marshallton and the community of Crooked Oak near the Mississippi border, close to the Tennessee River. For as long as Tallie could remember, Kingsley Woods had been a paradise for local sportsmen, hunters and fishermen alike. But Lobo Smothers, who lived in a shack deep in the woods on land his family had owned for generations, chose to desecrate the animal haven by hunting and trapping illegally for fun and profit.

Tallie and Susan crept through the dense forest of trees and underbrush, Solomon following their lead. For nearly two years, the sheriff's department had tried unsuccessfully to assist the game warden in catching Lobo Smothers in the act. Every lead came to a dead end. Every warning came too late. Lobo always seemed to be one step ahead, and Tallie figured that someone had to be tipping him off.

"Listen." Susan stopped dead still.

"Be quiet," Tallie said, issuing the warning to both Susan and Solomon.

Tallie crept closer to the sound, the rustling of leaves, the *cling-clang* of metal. When they neared a small clearing, Tallie and Susan hunkered down, hiding behind a tall hedge of wild bushes.

"It's him," Susan whispered.

Tallie saw Lobo Smothers, his broad back hunched over a metal trap. Sweat stains marred his blue chambray shirt. Long, matted strings of reddish-brown hair clung to his thick neck. It was all she could do not to run toward the man, screaming and hitting and venting her rage. This dirty, uneducated ruffian killed not only for the money but for the joy it gave him, totally unconcerned with the suffering of the poor animals who died slowly and painfully in his traps or the illegality of his actions.

"It makes me sick to my stomach just watching him setting that awful thing." Susan closed her eyes.

"I told you not to come, didn't I? I could have done this without you."

"I couldn't let you do this all alone," Susan said. "I may be squeamish, but I'm not a coward."

"You're just way too softhearted." Tallie laid her shotgun on the ground beside her, removed the camera hanging around her neck, released the lens cap and aimed directly at Lobo Smothers.

"You're as softhearted as I am."

"Yeah, but I grew up with a rough old grandfather and three big brothers, so I toughened up over the years, whereas you grew up with that spinster aunt of yours and all her animals." With her camera aimed, Tallie snapped picture after picture. She and Susan were secure in their position yards away from Lobo Smothers, the telephoto lens on Tallie's camera affording them the luxury of distance.

"What's he doing now?" Susan whispered, scratching her arm.

"The insects are pretty bad in here, aren't they?" Tallie replaced the camera strap around her neck. "He's finished here. He'll be moving on any minute now. Let's follow him and see what else he's up to."

"But you got the pictures of him setting that trap, didn't you?"

"Yeah, but I have a feeling he's going to be checking the traps he's already set." Grabbing Susan by the arm, Tallie helped her to her feet, then reached down to retrieve her shotgun. "Listen, if you don't think you can stomach seeing an animal caught in one of his traps, why don't you go back to the car and wait for me."

"No way! I'm going with you." Susan followed Tallie as faithfully as Solomon did. "If you get in trouble, I want to be there to help if I can."

"Do you really think he's going to check his other traps?"

"There's only one way to find out," Tallie said.

The two women followed a discreet distance behind, but Tallie had spent enough time in these woods when she was growing up to be able to keep track of Lobo without losing him and without alerting him to their presence.

Within five minutes, Lobo had stopped again. A small red fox, caught in one of Lobo's vicious traps, had obviously tried to gnaw off his trapped hind leg before he'd died. The sight of the poor little animal turned Tallie's stomach. She closed her eyes to block out the sight.

"Don't look, Susan."

"Oh, dear Lord," Susan moaned, then stepped backward, pressing her hands against a nearby tree as she gagged.

Solomon, standing alert beside Tallie, turned toward Susan when Tallie watched her friend closely. She'd known it was a mistake allowing Susan to come with her. Susan just wasn't cut out for the gritty reality of life.

"Are you all right?"

"Take pictures," Susan whispered. "Don't worry about me." Clutching her stomach, Susan doubled over. Bending down on her knees, she vomited.

Tallie crept closer to where Lobo was removing his catch from the trap. *Snap. Snap. Snap.* If this wasn't enough evidence for the game warden, then Tallie didn't know what it would take to put Lobo behind bars.

She couldn't wait to see Lowell Redman's face when she showed him the pictures. And just imagine what Peyton would say when she showed him. Wrong, Tallie! You won't be showing anything to Peyton. He's out of your life now.

It's what he wants and it's what you want. You both agreed. Remember?

"Is he gone?" Susan asked when she returned to Tallie's side.

"Yeah, I figure he's going to keep moving from trap to trap."

"Are we going to keep following him?"

"Just to one more trap," Tallie said.

"I didn't see where he went." Susan glanced all around. "Do you know the right direction?"

"He went east. Come on."

It didn't take Tallie long to realize that she'd lost Lobo, that somewhere along the way, he'd reversed his steps. Was it possible, she wondered, that he knew he was being followed? Lobo might be uneducated, but he wasn't ignorant, at least not when it came to Kingsley Woods, to hunting and fishing and trapping and keeping one step ahead of the law.

"What's wrong?" Susan asked when Tallie stopped near a rotting log.

"He's disappeared. He could have heard us or spotted us or just sensed he was being followed."

"What are we going to do?"

"We're going to get the hell out of Dodge." Tallie grinned at her friend, but realized her humor had been lost on the ashen-faced Susan.

"Do you think he'll come after us?" Susan rubbed her hands up and down her jean-covered hips.

"I doubt it," Tallie lied.

Within a few minutes, they'd made their way back to the scene of the newly set trap. Both of them out of breath from running, they paused momentarily.

Tallie heard Solomon growl. Jerking her head around, she saw Lobo Smothers braced against a huge oak tree, a self-satisfied smile on his dirty face.

"What are you two gals doing out in the woods?"

Susan grabbed Tallie's hand. "Tallie?"

"Enjoying the scenery," Tallie said.

"Taking some pictures?" Lobo pointed to the camera hanging around Tallie's neck. "You wouldn't of happened to've taken some pictures of me and my animal traps, would you?"

"I didn't think you set illegal animal traps." Tallie placed her hand on Solomon's neck, knowing full well that she might have to give her Great Dane an attack order at any moment. The shotgun she carried was loaded, but she intended to use it only as a last resort. It wasn't filled with birdshot, and if she aimed it at Lobo, she was likely to kill him.

"Just give me the camera and you gals can be on your way, all safe and sound." Taking a step away from the tree and toward Tallie and Susan, Lobo curved his lips into a snaggletoothed grin.

Tallie didn't want to relinquish the first real evidence anyone had ever gotten on this low-life scum, but there was a real possibility that he would try to harm them if they refused his request. Of course, they did have a couple of advantages. Solomon. And a loaded shotgun.

Tallie didn't realize what was happening until it was too late. Susan rushed forward, flinging herself at Lobo Smothers.

"Run, Tallie, run!" Susan screamed. "Don't let him have your camera."

Oh, hell's toenails! They were done for now, Tallie thought. Whatever had possessed Susan to act so foolhardily?

Lobo swung Susan around, gripping her by the waist and lifting her off the ground. His grin widened into a vicious smirk. "Yeah, Tallie, go ahead and run. Take your little camera and leave your friend behind. I've been wanting to get to know Miss Susan for years now. By the time you get back with help, me and Miss Susan will have become mighty close friends.''

Tallie swallowed hard. Lobo had her over a barrel. She knew it and so did he. "Let her go, and I'll give you the camera.''

"No!'' Susan screamed, struggling in Lobo's grasp. "Don't you dare give him—''

Lobo covered her mouth with his hand, then screeched like a stuck hog when she bit him. In that split second of pain, Lobo released Susan. Tallie gave Solomon the attack order and both she and the Great Dane dived forward, right into Lobo. Susan fell to the ground, rolling over and over, getting as far away as she could.

Solomon attacked, knocking Lobo to the ground. When Tallie thought Lobo was subdued enough to listen to reason, she called off Solomon, then pointed her shotgun in the center of Lobo's chest.

"Susan, you're going to have to go for help while I keep Mr. Smothers occupied.''

"I can't leave you here alone with that man.''

"Susan, go for help. Now!''

Instantly obeying, Susan fled thought the woods.

Peyton and Lowell saw Susan Williams as she came flying out of the woods into the clearing by the old campsite where they'd parked the sheriff's car beside Tallie's Camaro.

She ran straight into Lowell's arms. He held her, rubbing her back, trying to soothe her.

"Where's Tallie?'' Peyton asked.

Pulling free from Lowell, Susan faced Peyton. "She's holding her shotgun on Lobo Smothers. Out there in the woods.''

"Show us where,'' Peyton said.

"I think I can take y'all straight to her." Susan tugged on Peyton's hand. "I ran as fast as I could to get back to the car to go for help, and I tried to memorize the path I took."

Peyton and Lowell followed Susan into Kingsley Woods, Lowell removing his 9mm automatic from his hip holster. When they were deep into the forest, Susan began to call Tallie's name. Within minutes, Tallie answered.

"I'm over here, Susan. I'm fine. Have you already called for help this quick?"

"Lowell and Peyton are with me," Susan said as they came into the clearing. "They'd just driven up to the campsite when I got back to your car."

If Peyton hadn't been scared for Tallie and infuriated at her for doing something so totally foolish, he would have found the scene before him quite amusing—almost as amusing as Sheriff Redman found it.

Lobo Smothers, all six-feet-four inches of him, lay flat on his back on the ground. Solomon's front paws rested on Lobo's neck, and Tallie held her shotgun an inch away from his stomach.

"How'd you know where we were?" Tallie asked, stealing a quick glance at Peyton before returning her full attention to Lobo.

"Sheila called. She was worried about you and Susan." Peyton had never before known the mixture of emotions that were stirring around inside him at this precise moment. Fear, anger and passion were a deadly combination.

"She didn't have to call you. We took care of everything ourselves." After lifting her shotgun from Lobo's stomach, she ordered Solomon up. "I'll turn Mr. Smothers over to you, Lowell." She held her shotgun in one hand. "And I've got some pictures here that I think you and the game warden will be interested in." She patted the camera hanging around her neck.

"Well, I'll be damned." Lowell shook his head. "Get up, Lobo. I'm going to give you a free ride to jail. You've got a lot of questions to answer."

Lobo made no protest when Lowell escorted him out of the woods, his hands cuffed behind him. Peyton zeroed in on Tallie, grabbing her by the shoulders.

"What the hell did you think you were doing, coming out here like this? Lobo could have killed you and Susan."

"He didn't, did he?" Tallie jerked away from Peyton. "We're both just fine, aren't we, Susan?"

"I'm going to ride back into town with Lowell," Susan said. "If you want to give me the camera, I'll see that Lowell gets the film and I'll answer any questions he might have."

"There's no need," Tallie said. "We can ride into town together."

"Give me the camera, Tallie." Peyton lifted the camera from around Tallie's neck. "I'll drive you and Susan into town, and then you and I are going to have a long, over-due talk."

"About what?" Tallie allowed Peyton to take the camera.

"About why you can't seem to stay out of trouble, and why I can't seem to stay out of your life."

Evening shadows fell across Tallie's front yard, the sun lying in the lavender sky like a scoop of orange sherbet on a pastel plate. Tallie pulled the Camaro up in the driveway, got out and slammed the door. Peyton followed her, parking his Jag directly behind her car.

Tallie stomped up the porch steps, not waiting for Peyton. By the time he'd gotten out of his car, she was unlocking her front door.

"There's no need to run," Peyton called out when she raced into the living room, the storm door banging behind her. "I'm not leaving. Not until we've settled things once and for all."

Tallie flung her shoulder purse and her camera bag down on the coffee table. Then she unloaded her shotgun and laid it and the shells on the dining-room table as she passed through the room on her way to the kitchen.

Peyton caught up with her in front of the sink where she was filling a glass with tap water. He stood directly behind her, but didn't touch her.

"Go away, Peyt. I thought we'd already settled things once and for all. I thought we did that the other night at the Pale Rider."

"Yeah, I thought so, too, but I was mistaken."

"No, you weren't mistaken." Tallie lifted the glass to her mouth, took several deep swallows, then placed the glass in the sink. She turned to face Peyton. "Things were settled. They are settled. Nobody asked you to come charging out to Kingsley Woods to save me, did they? No! I sure as hell didn't ask for your help this time."

"Are you saying that when you told Sheila Vance where you and Susan were going, you didn't even once consider the possibility that she'd call me?"

"Of course not! I...well, I don't think I did. Did I? Oh, I don't know anymore. Maybe I did. Maybe that's the reason I told her. I have no idea. I'm totally confused when it comes to you and me."

"You think you're confused? How do you think I feel?" He took her shoulders in his grasp, holding her with gentle force. "My life is a total mess when you're in it, but I've found out that it's not worth much without you."

"Please, Peyt, don't say things now you're going to regret tomorrow. Nothing has changed between us. I'm still who I am, and you're still who you are. I want a small town, a simple, uncomplicated life. You want to live in Nashville and run the whole state."

"Tallie Bishop, you live the most complicated life of any woman I know, small town or not."

Tallie knew she had to escape from Peyton, from the firm, possessive hold of his hands, from the hot, predatory look of passion she saw in his eyes. Somehow, his fear for her safety and his anger over her impulsiveness had combined with the passion he'd held in check for so many years. If she couldn't stop him now, there would be no stopping him later.

Tallie placed her hands atop Peyton's, where they rested on her shoulders. "I want you to leave, Peyton. Now."

"You want me to leave?"

"Yes."

"I can't do that."

She jerked his hands from her shoulders and moved away from him. He grabbed her by the wrist.

Pausing in her flight, caught by his tight hold and by the pleading look on his face, Tallie faced him. "I can take care of myself. You saw that today, didn't you? I don't know if I told Sheila where Susan and I were going because subconsciously I wanted you to come to my rescue or not. Maybe I did. But the bottom line is this, I can survive without you."

"Can you, Tallie? Can you really?" He pulled her to him, slowly, one small tug at a time, until her body touched his. "Well, I found out something today, Tallulah Bankhead Bishop. I can't survive without you."

She stared at him, unable to believe what he'd just said to her. "You don't mean that."

"I do mean it, Tallie." Holding her to him, one arm wrapped securely around her waist, he raised his other hand to touch her face. "I'm as confused about us as you are. I don't know if we have a prayer of making things work for us. All I know is that I'm tired of fighting the desire I feel for you. I'm tired of protecting myself from you and I'm tired of protecting you from me."

"Oh, Peyt." She understood only too well what he was telling her. It was now or never. If she turned him away this time, they wouldn't get another chance.

"You're all I think about, sugar. Day and night. You're the first thing I think about when I get up every morning, and your face haunts me when I close my eyes at night."

With the utmost tenderness, he stroked her cheek with his fingertips. "I want you, Tallie. I want you like I've never wanted anything in my life."

Tears welled up in her eyes, caught in her throat and tightened her heart. He hadn't said he loved her, had made no promises beyond the moment, but she realized he was being as honest with himself and with her as he knew how to be.

"I've never wanted anyone else but you, Peyt. Only you. Always you." She surrendered herself to him, giving him the right to take her and make her his. It was all she'd ever wanted.

Taking her face in both hands, he drew her lips to his, kissing her with tender passion. She swayed toward him, slipping her arms around his waist, urging him closer. He ran his hands down her throat, across her shoulders and arms, then pulled her into his embrace, positioning her body intimately against his.

Their kiss deepened, intensifying until Tallie opened her mouth to give him entrance. He swept his hands over her body as if he longed to memorize each and every curve. His tongue plunged and stroked and tasted. Moaning with pleasure, she rubbed against him, seeking a closer contact, wanting to be a part of this big, overpowering man she loved.

Peyton lifted Tallie into his arms. She clung to him, her arms draped around his neck. Closing her eyes, she sighed deeply as he carried her out of the kitchen and down the hall to her bedroom. The door stood open, a lamp on the bedside table casting a warm, inviting glow across the room.

"I've had dreams about this, you know," he admitted, laying her down on the plaid coverlet. "Laying you down, covering you with my body, stripping away your clothes, kissing every inch of—"

Reaching up, she covered his lips with her finger. "Lawyers talk too much." She smiled at him when he looked into her eyes. "You don't have to convince me. You've already got me."

"Do you want less talk and more action, sugar?" Lying down beside her on the bed, he propped himself on his elbow, leaned over her and began to unbutton her shirt. "I have no idea what you like in a lover. Tell me what you want, Tallie, and whatever it is, I'll do it."

"I...I'm not sure." Didn't he know that she'd had no other lover, that he was the first and only man she'd ever loved? "All I know is that I want *you*, Peyt."

"I'll make it perfect for you, sugar. I promise."

One by one, he removed the garments from her body. Her shirt. Her bra. His hands caressed, his lips consumed. Her jeans fell to the floor, followed by her panties. While he suckled her breasts, he eased his hands down her hips, lifting her up to meet the hard, aching part of him encased in briefs and slacks. He throbbed with desire, with the need to be buried deep inside this beautiful woman.

But he would not rush her. He'd promised to make it perfect for her, and that's what he was going to do, even if it killed him in the process. He wanted their lovemaking to obliterate from her mind any experience that had come before, any man who'd ever known the pleasures of her body.

Tallie tugged his shirt free from his slacks, then with awkward fingers, she unbuttoned and removed the soft silk shirt from his body, tossing it on the floor. She ran her hands over his chest, his wide, hairy, heavily muscled chest. She slid her fingers into the thick mat of light brown hair that covered him from armpit to armpit, narrowing only slightly when it delved beneath his slacks.

She fumbled with his belt buckle, but couldn't manage to release it. She groaned in frustration. Peyton covered her eager hands with his.

"Not yet, sugar."

"But, Peyt . . . please."

"You're not ready yet."

"I am."

"You're not hot enough, sugar. Not wet enough. Not hungry and hurting enough." Sliding his hand between her legs, he sought and found her tiny nub of desire. When he petted her, she cried out, lifting herself up to meet his hand. "But you'll be ready when I take you. You'll be more than ready."

Tallie grabbed for him. He took her hands, lifted them above her head and held them down. "I knew you'd be eager, that you'd go about loving the way you do everything else in life. Ah, Tallie, Tallie. My sweet, beautiful Tallie."

He kissed her, forcefully and with great longing, plunging into her mouth, substituting this act for the more intimate one that he was deliberately postponing. When Tallie bucked up off the bed, rubbing herself against him, twining her legs around his thighs, Peyton felt himself tightening, a wildfire igniting inside him, burning him with his own passion.

He broke the kiss, nipping at her chin, her neck, the tip of her ear. "That's it, my little heathen. Feel the need. Want me. Want me desperately."

"I do," she moaned when his mouth covered her breast, his lips pulling on the nipple, his tongue stroking her. "No, please . . . please . . ."

Tallie had no idea how long Peyton lingered over each tingling part of her body. She had lost track of time, even of reality. Her whole world consisted of nothing more than

Peyton Rand and the delicious feelings his magic touch created within her.

Hotter and brighter and all-consuming, the fire of passion burned within him. He made love to Tallie as he had never made love to another woman, with all the desperate longing he'd held in check for so many years. He'd never known anything like this—and he knew he never would again, not with any other woman. Only with Tallie. His Tallie.

When he spread her legs and lifted her hips in his big hands, Tallie cried out, uncertain what was happening. And then his mouth touched her, and she melted. Hot and sweet and dripping with desire. Peyton brought her to the brink of completion. She clutched at his shoulders, her short nails biting into his flesh, grasping at his hard muscles. With one final stroke, he toppled her over the brink. Groaning, gasping and finally crying, Tallie trembled with release.

"You're ready now, sugar." With great urgency, he shed his slacks and briefs, kicking off his leather loafers and tossing his socks on the floor.

He hovered over her as satiation claimed her. "Peyton?"

"That's only the beginning. Now I make you mine." He kissed her quickly, with demanding force. "You want to be mine, don't you, Tallie?"

"Yes. Oh, yes."

With one deep, hard plunge he entered her. She cried out from the unexpected pain and the incredible feeling of completion. Peyton stopped, his whole body trembling with the effort to remain perfectly still.

"Tallie?"

She knew what he was asking her. If she admitted the truth, would he stop loving her? "Please don't stop, don't ever stop loving me."

"I don't want to hurt you, sugar."

"You'll hurt me if you stop, if you don't make me yours."

Slowly, with great tenderness, he moved deeper, then retreated. She clung to him, encouraging him with her touch. He delved in and out repeatedly, slowly and gently at first, then gradually increasing the speed and force.

He was fast losing control, but so was she. Tallie, his wild little heathen, took all that he gave her and returned full measure, asking for more, demanding every last ounce of strength and power and manliness he possessed.

She tightened around him, grasping him to her, claiming all that he was. And he gave himself over to her, wanting to hold back, to wait, but unable to resist the overwhelming power she wielded over him.

Fast and hot and undeniable, her climax gripped her only moments after Peyton fell apart in her arms, his big body erupting in spasms of release. Trembling with passionate force, she clung to him, riding out the aftershocks, accepting every tiny remaining quiver of completion.

Sliding off her, onto the bed by her side, he gathered her into his arms, holding her to him with a possessiveness he'd never known. She was his. His woman. Now and forever.

"I love you, Peyt," she whispered, her head resting on his shoulder, her lips against his neck. "I've never loved anyone but you."

"I don't deserve you, sugar. You're too good, too honest for a man like me."

Snuggling against him, she laid her hand on his chest, curling his chest hair around her fingers. "Oh, I think you just might deserve me. I have a feeling that the good Lord decided I was just what you need and that's why he threw us together and kept us together all these years."

"We'll work out all the details of this relationship later, sugar. Right now, I don't want to think anymore. All I want to do is feel."

Tallie crawled over on top of him, rubbing against him like a sultry little kitten. "Do you feel that?"

Grasping her hips in his hands, he positioned her over his renewed arousal, lifting himself up and into her. "Do you feel that, sugar?"

She laughed aloud, glorying in the passion that flowed between them like a raging river out of bounds and way beyond human control.

Eight

Peyton lay with his back braced against the headboard, cushioned with two feather pillows. Tallie lay against him, her head snuggled to his side. He'd been watching her for quite some time, awed by her beauty and innocence, filled with emotions he'd never known he possessed. She was his now, as surely as he was hers. There could be no turning back, no running away, no denying that Tallie Bishop was a part of his life. No, not just a part of his life—she was a part of him.

Did he love her? He didn't know. He wasn't even sure he was capable of love, the kind of love a woman like Tallie needed and deserved. He had spent most of his life centered on what he thought was expected of him, trying to decide on what was the best course of action to take in order to achieve his goals.

He supposed he'd been considering political office for years, the need as deeply entrenched in him as his desire for Tallie. Was it possible for him to have both? Could he continue his affair with Tallie and accept his party's nomination for governor?

Tallie moaned in her sleep, cuddling against him, her small hand instinctively reaching out for him. He laid his hand over hers where it rested on his stomach.

An affair? With this woman? Tallie was the marrying kind, the white-picket-fence-and-babies kind. Maybe he should marry her. He knew he'd never find another woman he wanted more, but could she adapt to his life-style? Should he expect her to change her whole life to suit him?

Tallie opened her eyes to find Peyton looking down at her, a warm smile on his face. Lifting herself, she slipped her arms around him, her mouth seeking his. She kissed him with sweet, morning-after happiness. He returned the kiss.

"No regrets?" he asked.

"No regrets. Not ever. Last night—" She blushed. She shook her head, swinging her short, black curls "—and this morning were perfect. More perfect than I'd ever dreamed making love could be."

"I've been thinking."

"A dangerous enterprise for a lawyer." Giggling, she dotted light, damp kisses across his shoulder.

"Behave yourself, sugar. We need to talk. Serious talk." He lifted her away from him, placing several inches between their bodies.

What was he going to tell her? That it had been great, but it was over, that he had his future to consider and she just didn't fit in? "Uh-oh. Maybe I should ask if you have any regrets?"

"My only regret is that we waited so long to make love."

When she reached for him, he grabbed her hands. "Serious talk first."

Laying her hands in her lap, she nodded agreement. "I'm listening."

"We've already agreed that you and I are the mismatch of the century, so there's no need to rehash all our differences."

"Agreed. I think we have more in common than either of us ever realized." Tallie grinned.

"Don't change the subject." He smiled back at her. "The facts are that I'm a wealthy lawyer who is making plans to run for governor. That's who I am, Tallie."

"I would never ask you to give up your dream." A spiral of fear curled inside her stomach.

"You see, sugar, the problem is that I'm a selfish bastard. I always have been." When he heard her gasp and knew she was going to protest, he held up his hand, motioning for her to stay quiet. "I don't want to give up my plans for a political career, but I don't want to give you up, either."

"Oh." She understood his predicament only too well. She and politics would mix like oil and water.

"I'm not making any promises or offering you anything, but I think we owe it to ourselves to give our relationship a chance, to see if we can make it work."

"What are you suggesting?"

"I want us to start dating, to go out and be seen together as a couple." He searched her face for some clue as to how she felt about what he'd just said. Her face was a complete blank. "I'll make an announcement to the effect that you and I are...dating."

"It probably wouldn't be a good idea to say that we're lovers. People might get the wrong idea."

"Tallie, I know how you feel about pretending, about presenting—"

"About lying."

"Okay, about lying. Look, sugar, I'm not asking you to change the person you are to make things easier for me. This trial period isn't going to work unless you and I both just be ourselves, but I am willing to compromise on a few issues if you are.''

"Trial period?'' Tallie pulled the sheet up to cover her naked breasts.

Peyton jerked the sheet back down. "Don't get all huffy and defensive. This is a trial period for me just as much as for you. It's a trial period for our relationship, to see if it's possible for us to have a future together.''

"I see.'' She wasn't sure she liked the idea. After all, she was in love. She didn't need a trial period. But Peyton did. He had a great deal more to lose than she did; all she had to lose was her heart.

"We'll start this Friday night. I've got to attend a little get-together given by one of the party's biggest supporters. I want you to go with me.''

"What? I can't. I don't know anything about—''

The phone rang. Tallie jumped out of bed, picked up Peyton's silk shirt from the floor, slipped into it and raced out of the bedroom and down the hall.

Peyton got up, pulled on his slacks and walked down the hall to find Tallie in the living room.

"It's Spence.'' She handed Peyton the telephone.

"What's up?'' Peyton asked. "How did you know where to find me?''

"You haven't seen the morning paper, have you?'' Spence asked.

"No, why?''

"If you had, you wouldn't ask how I knew where you were.''

"Tell it to me gently.'' Peyton sat down on the sofa.

Tallie sat down beside him. "What's wrong?''

"Go outside and get your morning paper,'' Peyton told her.

"Why?'' she asked as she stood up, then walked to the front door.

"Tallie's going to get the paper. We'll see soon enough, so go ahead and tell me." Peyton leaned back into the sofa, crossing one leg over the other at his knee.

"Someone took it upon themselves to share your and Tallie's little adventure in Kingsley Woods yesterday with a reporter from the *Marshallton News*. You're not front page, but you're page one in regional news."

Tallie came running back into the house, the newspaper in her hands folded back, sections of it hanging loosely from her fingers. "Is Peyton Rand trying to prove to the voters of Tennessee that he's just an old-fashioned knight in shining armor by his continuous rescues of the young and beautiful Crooked Oak tow-truck driver, Tallulah Bishop? Although Mr. Rand claims that he and Ms. Bishop are only acquaintances—"

"Enough!" Peyton said, interrupting Tallie's reading aloud. "Thanks for calling, Spence. We'll talk later."

"What do you think is going to happen if you announce that we're dating?" Tallie flung the paper to the floor.

"I've changed my mind. I'm not going to announce anything."

"I suppose it was just wishful thinking on our parts—"

"There will be reporters at the party Friday, outside waiting for a story and a few invited inside for scoops on the political scene. They'll see us arrive together and they're bound to ask questions. We'll answer their questions. Truthfully." Peyton grabbed her around the waist, toppling her over onto his lap.

"Truthfully?" Tallie laid her hand on his chest. "You're going to tell them that we're lovers?"

"We're going to say that we're good friends, that we're dating, that we are seriously involved."

"Seriously involved? They'll take that to mean—"

"That we're seriously involved," he said.

"Are we—" The sharp ring of the telephone jarred Tallie. "Good grief. What now?"

"I'll get it." Peyton reached out to answer the phone.

Tallie shook her head. "No, I'll get it." When he looked at her with puzzlement in his eyes, she said, "How would you explain to someone what you're doing at my house so early on Sunday morning?"

"I'd tell them that I'd been here all night making mad, passionate love to you."

Tallie couldn't keep from smiling. The phone continued ringing. She picked up the receiver. "Hello."

"This is Lowell Redman, I just wanted to let you know that Lobo Smothers is out on bail. I don't think there's anything to worry about, but I thought you should know. We'll keep an eye on him."

"Thanks for calling." She knew that Peyton was watching and listening, that he would want to know who the caller was.

"I've tried to get in touch with Peyton this morning, but I keep getting his answering machine. If you see him, tell him to give me a call."

"Yes, well . . . if I see him, I'll tell him."

Peyton reached around her, placing his hand over the telephone mouthpiece. "Who is it, Tallie? Is it someone looking for me?"

She tried to pull the receiver away from Peyton, but he grabbed it from her. "Peyton Rand here."

"Ah . . . yeah, Peyt, is that you?" Lowell stammered.

"What's up? Is there some problem I should know about?" Peyton watched Tallie place her hands on her hips and glare at him.

"I just told Tallie that Lobo Smothers is out on bail. What I didn't tell her was that he was running his mouth off how she and Susan were going to be sorry they'd ever messed with him. I warned him that if he went anywhere near either of them, he'd be back in jail so fast it'd make his head spin."

"Damn that man! I'd like to see him behind bars and out of Tallie's life." Peyton frowned at Tallie, giving her a warning look.

"There's more," Lowell said. "I just didn't want to worry Tallie, but you need to know. Cliff Nolan showed up in town last night. He was drunk, wrecked his car and spent the night at the hospital. We can keep him in jail for a few days, but that's about it."

"You're just full of good news this morning, aren't you, old buddy?" Peyton didn't want to think about the threat both of these men posed for Tallie, but he realized that he couldn't allow her to dismiss the danger, which he knew she'd try to do. "Thanks, Lowell. You do what you can at your end and I'll take care of things here."

Peyton replaced the receiver. "Go pack a bag. You're coming to Jackson with me."

"What?"

"You heard me. You're staying with me until we can be sure you aren't in any danger."

"Now, you wait just one darn minute." Tallie walked over to Peyton. Looking up at him, she pointed her finger in his face. "I can't move in with you. We're just dating. Remember? I can handle Lobo Smothers if he comes around. It's warm enough for Solomon to sleep out on the porch like he did last night. He's a good watchdog."

"All right, if you won't move in with me, I'll stay here with you." Peyton grabbed Tallie's finger, playfully biting the tip.

"No, you won't stay here." She jerked her hand away from him. "We're just starting our trial period, testing the waters with our relationship and ... and with the public— the people who have the power to make or break your political career."

"So, if we're living together, we can speed up the process a little."

"Peyt, the one thing you're going to have to get used to about me is that I have a mind of my own."

He guffawed. "You really think I don't already know that?"

"I will not allow you to run my life, to make my decisions. No matter how much I love you, I won't let you tell me what I can and cannot do. Is that understood?" She was in front of him, her finger pointed directly in his face again.

"Get that damned finger out of my face, or so help me, Tallulah, I'll bite it off!"

She dropped her hand, gazing up at him with a mixture of determination and feminine pride glowing in her eyes. "I'll get Susan to come out and spend a few days with me. Yesterday you saw how well the two of us can handle things."

Peyton groaned, knowing full well when he was defeated. "Oh, yeah, you and Susan can conquer the world."

Tallie slipped her arms around Peyton's neck. "Susan and I will spend the next five nights over at Sheila's. I'll take my shotgun and Solomon."

"Three women alone together."

"I'll have a gun. Sheila will have a gun. Solomon can sleep outside. And Mike's trailer is just down the road." Standing on tiptoe, Tallie nuzzled his chin with her nose. "Agree to my terms and I'll go to that stupid political get-together with you Friday night."

"That's blackmail, sugar."

"How can you say that? I'm simply making you an offer you can't refuse."

"I'll accept your offer because I don't have any other choice." He pulled her up into his arms, his head lowering, his lips brushing hers, their breaths mingling. "I want you to tell me that you're aware of how dangerous Lobo Smothers and Cliff Nolan can be."

"I'm not stupid, Peyt." Tallie kissed him. Quick. Hard. Tempting. "I'm not going to take any chances. I promise I'll stay out of trouble."

"I'm driving out here every night to see you. If you won't let me stay here, I'll stay over in Marshallton with Spence and Pattie."

"After the party next Friday night...if everything works out okay and everybody knows we're seriously involved, then maybe we could..."

"Are you saying I can spend the night again?"

"I'm saying that after your highfalutin political buddies meet me in a social setting and they all know that we're...dating...well, if after that, you still want me and think we—"

He didn't give her a chance to finish before crushing his lips to hers, kissing her with all the passion and tempest raging inside him. He wanted this woman. He wanted her now. Lifting her into his arms, he laid her down on the sofa and began unbuttoning his shirt that she was wearing, pulling it away from her body to reveal the beauty of her naked flesh.

"Peyton?"

"If we're not going to make love for another five days, then let's not waste the rest of today talking."

Tallie unzipped his slacks when he leaned down over her. "You've learned fast, haven't you, Counselor, that actions speak louder than words?"

Thursday afternoon, Tallie waited patiently in the teacher's lounge at Marshallton Community College. Both Susan and Sheila, with whom she'd spent the last few nights, thought she'd been out of her mind when she'd called Donna Fields and asked for her help.

"It's like asking the enemy for advice on how to win a battle," Sheila had said.

"Donna Fields is not my enemy," Tallie had assured her friend. "I don't want Peyton to be ashamed of me when he takes me to that party Friday night. Donna is the perfect person to give me pointers on how to dress, how to act, what to expect."

The past week had been one of the best weeks of Tallie's life. She was gloriously, insanely in love with Peyton Rand, and she no longer had to pretend she wasn't. He had called her two or three times every day and taken her out to dinner every night.

They hadn't made love again, even though Peyton had been less than understanding about her reasons for wanting to wait. It wasn't that she didn't want him as much as he wanted her. It was just that, for her own sake, for the sake of her sanity, she had to make sure that their relationship had a fighting chance. She figured they'd both know where they stood after tomorrow night's big shindig.

"Tallie?" Donna Fields stood in the doorway, a warm, friendly smile on her lovely face.

"I certainly appreciate your doing this for me, Donna. I guess most people wouldn't understand why I asked you for help, considering the fact that you and Peyt...well, that you two were an item for a while."

"Would you care for some tea?" Donna asked as she filled her cup with water from the bottled jug on the counter.

"No, thanks."

Donna placed the cup in the microwave. "Peyt and I were and are good friends, but we were never really an item, except in the newspapers."

"Pattie told me the night I met you that you weren't my competition."

"She was right." Donna removed an Earl Grey tea bag from a box on a top shelf above the microwave. "I knew before you and I met that Peyton was in love with you."

"Oh, but he isn't...I mean he hasn't told me that... I'm talking too much."

Donna smiled, the expression turning her face from delicate loveliness to absolute beauty. "Give him a little more time, Tallie, and as soon as he figures it out for himself, he'll tell you he loves you. Peyton is a very smart man, but he doesn't know the first thing about love."

"He grew up in a house without love, in a family with other priorities."

"If he's taking you to Harold and Betty Glover's party, then Peyton has his priorities straight. Harold is a man with enough money and power to hand Peyton their party's nomination for governor."

When the microwave beeped, Donna removed her cup, dropped in the tea bag and waited for the mixture to brew.

"So you're saying that if I screw up, I could lose Peyton the nomination?" Tallie wiped her sweaty palms on her jeans.

"That's not what I'm saying at all." Picking up her teacup, Donna motioned toward the small sofa in the corner of the room. "Let's sit. I have the next hour free."

"Peyton and I have agreed to a trial relationship, to see if we can make it work, if there's a chance we could have a future together." Tallie sat down beside Donna.

"I see." Donna sipped her tea, then placed the cup on the round table to her right. "And this trial period was Peyton's idea?"

"In a way, but it was really a mutual decision. If I can make Friday night work, then I've got a real chance with Peyton. That's why I want you to help me."

"What do you want me to do?"

"I know this may sound crazy, but what do I wear?"

Donna laughed. "It doesn't sound crazy at all. It's a typical feminine question."

"Well?"

"This event will be fairly formal, so you'll need something very dressy." Donna surveyed Tallie from head to toe. "Tell me what sort of dress you'd feel comfortable and confident wearing, something strictly Tallie Bishop style."

"I look good in black," Tallie said. "And I've got a pretty decent figure, so I suppose I could wear something body-hugging, but classy."

"Sounds perfect. Do you have a dress like that?"

"No, but I could go to Jackson later and see if I can find something I can afford."

"Go to Justine's. I'll give you the address later. Just tell her that I sent you. She'll help you find the perfect dress at the right price." Donna lifted her teacup off the table. "What else do you need help with to make tomorrow night a success?"

"I have a reputation for talking first and thinking later, for taking action before I consider the consequences. I don't want to embarrass Peyton by saying or doing the wrong thing."

"Tallie, you can't go to this party and pretend to be someone you're not." Donna sipped her tea. "You're warm and caring and sensitive. I believe you'll be Peyton's greatest asset when he runs for governor."

"How can you possibly say that? Can you honestly see me as the first lady of Tennessee?"

"Yes, I can," Donna said, placing her teacup back on the table. "Peyton has everything going for him. Wealth, breeding, a highly successful law practice, a political family background and the drive and determination to fight against all the odds until he wins. But he lives in constant fear of becoming a replica of his father, of being as ruthless and self-serving as Marshall Rand was."

"You really do know Peyton quite well, don't you?" Tallie hated herself for feeling so jealous of Donna Fields, of the very fact that she knew the torment in Peyton's soul.

"There's no denying that Peyton is his father's son," Donna said. "He'll be the first to admit it. The only thing keeping Peyton from running for governor, from winning the election and being the best governor this state has ever had is his own fear."

"I don't understand what this has to do with your thinking I could be his first lady."

"Don't you understand?" Donna took Tallie's hand. "You, Tallie Bishop, with your honesty, your integrity, your true concern for others could well be Peyton's salvation."

"I'm not sure what you mean."

"With you at his side, he would never have to worry about becoming the kind of politician, the kind of man his father was. He would have to live up to your expectations. He'd see the world through your eyes."

Tallie choked back tears, the pain in her chest forcing her silence when she so badly wanted to speak, to tell Donna Fields that she understood.

"Your loving Peyton isn't bad for him," Donna said. "You see that now, don't you? You can go to the party with him tomorrow night and know that all you have to do is be yourself and you'll be an asset to Peyton and his career."

Tallie swallowed hard, blinking away the tears in her eyes. "I just hope Peyton realizes how lucky he is to have a friend like you."

"And I hope he realizes how lucky he is to have a woman who loves him enough to save him from himself," Donna told Tallie.

Nine

Betty and Harold Glover were old money, each with a Confederate colonel ancestor and a restored home dating back to the 1830s. Everyone knew Harold was one of the wealthiest and most influential men in the state.

So it's no wonder I'm nervous as a cat in a roomful of rocking chairs, Tallie thought as the parking attendant opened the door of Peyton's Jag and assisted her out onto the brick driveway. Within moments, Peyton took her arm and led her up the stairs to the front portico.

"Calm down, sugar. Everything's going to be just fine."

Glancing over at Peyton while squeezing his arm tightly, Tallie sucked in a deep breath of fresh night air. She'd never seen Peyton looking more handsome, more distinguished, more the successful Southern gentleman. Wearing a black tuxedo and white pleated shirt with black accessories, Peyton looked like a model out of the pages of *GQ*.

She didn't realize that she'd halted directly in front of the open double doors until Peyton gave her a gentle nudge.

"These people are my friends and associates, sugar. They're not a den of lions ready to devour you the minute we walk in and say good evening."

"Right," Tallie said. Straightening her shoulders, she tilted her chin, gave Peyton her most brilliant smile and stepped forward.

When they entered the throng of Tennessee's elite, Tallie's steps faltered. Enough of this nonsense, she told herself. You're Tallulah Bankhead Bishop and you're as good as anybody. Peyt's counting on you tonight. Don't try to be somebody you're not, but be on your best behavior.

Lowering his head, Peyton whispered, "Did I tell you how incredibly beautiful you look tonight?"

Leaning slightly against him, she nodded. "Yes, but I'm glad you told me again."

Peyton led her past several people talking together in small conversation groups, nodding greetings to some, exchanging a quick handshake with others, introducing Tallie whenever they paused long enough to do more than say hello.

Although Peyton felt a certain sense of apprehension about how people in general would react to his relationship with Tallie, his biggest worry was how Tallie would react if she picked up any reluctance to accept her from his friends and acquaintances.

Watching the way the men in the room stared at Tallie, Peyton's male ego swelled considerably. Not only did he know that his date was the sexiest, most beautiful woman in the room, but all the other men did, too. She looked elegant yet sensual in the floor-length, body-hugging black silk dress she wore. It was sleeveless and backless to the waist, its square neckline ending at her throat. The only jewelry she wore were a pair of small pearls that she'd told him had belonged to her Grandmother Bishop.

Tallie's head whirled with new names and new faces as she was introduced to person after person. She'd never shaken hands so many times in her life, and she'd never smiled so much. Champagne flowed like water—expensive champagne—but Tallie sipped on the same glass for over an hour. She was sure the food was delicious, but the knots in her stomach warned her she would regret eating anything.

"At last." Donna Fields placed her arm around Tallie's waist. "I've been trying to make my way over to see y'all for the past thirty minutes. Tallie, you look gorgeous!" She turned to Peyton. "You have told her how beautiful she looks, haven't you?"

"Oh, he's told me, all right," Tallie said. "He's told me so many times that I believe him."

Donna's friendly smile eased some of the tension churning inside Tallie. At least she knew for certain that she had one ally in the room besides Peyton.

"Have you introduced Tallie to Betty and Harold, yet?" Donna asked.

"We're working our way in that direction," Peyton said.

"Betty's daughter is visiting." Donna gave Peyton a strange look, one that Tallie interpreted to have a hidden meaning.

"Noreen is here?" The muscles in Peyton's face tightened. "I thought she was living in Atlanta since her divorce."

"Are y'all talking about Noreen Ellibee?" Tallie asked. "You two sure are acting funny. Is there something I should know?"

"Noreen is Betty Glover's daughter by her first husband," Peyton said. "She's a spoiled, selfish witch. And I used to date her."

"I remember. You were dating her when you first got out of law school." Tallie glanced at Donna and recognized the look for what it was—a warning. "Noreen could mean trouble for Peyton, for us. Right?"

"Betty had hoped her daughter would marry Peyton. A match made in Old South heaven." Donna gave Tallie's hand a comforting squeeze. "Noreen wanted Peyton and did everything in her power to get him, but—"

"But it didn't take me long to find out what sort of woman she was, and by the time we broke up, I felt nothing but contempt for her." Peyton slipped his arm around Tallie. "She has a vicious tongue, sugar, so watch yourself around her."

"Speak of the devil," Donna whispered under her breath when a tall, model-thin blonde approached, a phony million-dollar smile on her sharp-featured face.

"Peyton, honey-lamb, what on earth are you doing hiding yourself way over here?" Noreen sauntered up to Peyton, completely ignoring both Donna and Tallie. Lacing her arm around his, she pressed her breasts against him and leaned forward, her mouth touching his in a quick but passionate kiss.

Tallie stiffened. Well, well, well. She had expected a variety of interesting things to happen to her tonight, had even feared making a fool of herself, but she'd never once considered the possibility that she'd come face-to-face with a she-cat, a former girlfriend of Peyton's who apparently wanted to do battle in public.

Donna took Noreen by the arm, pulling her away from Peyton. "How nice to see you again, Noreen. Are you back home to stay or just for a short visit?"

Noreen's keen blue eyes fixed on Donna. "That depends." Noreen glanced from Donna to Peyton to Tallie and back to Donna. "Aren't you just an angel, Donna Fields, acting so brave and befriending your replacement when everyone knows your heart is broken." Before Donna had the chance to reply, Noreen whipped around to face Tallie. "And this must be *Sally*, the girl who's made such a name for herself with a shotgun."

Peyton tensed. He was going to put a stop to this right now. Of all the problems he had expected to face tonight, Noreen had not been one of them.

Tallie extended her hand. "I'm Tallulah Bishop, *Doreen*. I'm flattered that you seem to know so much about me. Do you keep informed about all the women in Peyton's life?"

"Just the ones who get their pictures plastered all over the newspapers and give Peyton such unfavorable publicity at a time when he needs to be courting the press." Noreen smiled triumphantly.

"Noreen." Peyton's tone warned the woman that she was overstepping the bounds.

"I'm not so sure the publicity Peyton and Tallie got was all bad," Donna said. "If you think about it, Peyton's defense of Tallie probably gave readers the idea that Peyton Rand is against wife beating and child abuse, and is definitely for animal rights, women's rights and law and order."

"I agree wholeheartedly." A short, balding man in his mid-seventies approached, a tall, slender woman on his arm. "At first, I thought the publicity this young lady was creating for our Peyton might hurt his chances of becoming governor, but I think Donna may be right."

"You can't mean to say that you'd approve of Peyton becoming involved with this . . . this tow-truck-driving redneck?" Noreen's hollow cheeks colored slightly, as much from having drunk one too many glasses of champagne as from agitation.

"Where are your manners, Noreen?" Betty Glover asked. "Miss Bishop is a guest here tonight."

Tallie wasn't quite sure what was happening, she just knew that she and Peyton and their little group had become the center of attention.

"Is there more than just friendship between you and Miss Bishop?" Harold Glover asked.

An attractive young reporter Tallie remembered from the day of her trial rooted his way into the group. "That's a question a lot of people would like to hear the answer to, Mr. Rand. If you run for governor, the woman at your side is going to be of prime interest to the people of Tennessee."

Noreen Ellibee's shrill laugh caught the attention of everyone close enough to hear. "You can't make a silk purse out this sow's ear. If you think for one minute that the people would accept her as the first lady, then you're not thinking with your head, you're thinking with your—"

"Noreen, that's quite enough!" Betty said.

"For the record," Peyton said, looking directly at Jeff Baines, the young reporter, "Tallulah Bishop is most definitely *the woman* in my life."

Harold reached out and took Tallie's limp hand. "Well, young lady, are you ready for this?"

"I'm not sure," Tallie said, overwhelmed by everything that had happened. Peyton had announced publicly that she was the woman in his life. But what exactly had he admitted to? That they were dating? That they were lovers?

"I've got my photographer here tonight, Mr. Rand. Would you and Miss Bishop mind posing for a few pictures?" Jeff asked.

"A couple of pictures," Peyton said. "But no more questions tonight."

Harold shook Tallie's hand heartily. "Good meeting you, young lady. Betty and I are looking forward to seeing more of you. Betty's on some committees you might be interested in. Animal rights, conservation, adult education. I have a feeling you might be just the thing these groups need to get them all stirred up, to help them accomplish more."

Betty nodded to Tallie. "I'll phone you next week, my dear, and we'll meet for lunch."

"Uh...thank you. Yes. That would be nice." Tallie had a notion that she felt pretty much the same as Alice had when she'd stepped through the looking glass.

As soon as the Glovers moved on, Donna slipped one of her arms around Tallie's waist and the other around Peyton. "I'd say, all things considered—" she eyed Noreen Ellibee several feet away, accepting another glass of champagne from the waiter "—tonight has been a success for the team of Rand and Bishop."

Just as Jeff Baines led his photographer over to Peyton and Tallie, a visibly inebriated Noreen pushed her way through the party crowd of observers. Donna gave Tallie and Peyton quick hugs, then stepped back to watch their triumph.

"Smile and act like you're happy," Peyton told Tallie as he put his arm around her waist and pulled her up against his side. "You're going to have to get used to this sort of thing."

The photographer aimed his camera. Tallie smiled. Peyton emitted his usual charisma. Noreen, swaying slightly on her feet, moved forward, her glass of champagne teetering in her unsteady hand.

"She must be damned good in bed," Noreen shouted. "I can't think of any other reason you'd be fool enough to risk everything for her."

In one unbelievable instant, Noreen lunged, Peyton threw up a protective hand to protect Tallie, accidently knocking Noreen's glass out of her hand and scraping the side of her mouth with his fist. Champagne splattered all over Tallie's new black silk dress. A trickle of blood oozed from Noreen's lip. And the entire scene was saved for posterity by the flash of a photographer's camera.

Peyton handed Tallie a cup of coffee, which she accepted without looking at him. She hadn't said more than a dozen words on the ride over to his apartment, and he knew full well that she was more than simply upset. How he handled things with her tonight would determine the outcome of their relationship. He was damned scared—scared he might lose Tallie.

"My robe's a little big on you." He sat beside her, placing his own coffee cup down on the glass table in front of the blue leather sofa.

Tallie tugged on the belt, which hung below her knees on both sides of the robe. "As soon as my dress is dry enough for me to put back on, I want you to take me home."

"Tonight was supposed to be our night," Peyton reminded her. "Holding you in my arms, making love to you all night is all I've thought about this week."

Tears welled up in Tallie's eyes. Being with Peyton, knowing the ecstasy she'd found in being his lover had been foremost in her mind all week. She had wanted desperately to be accepted by his friends and acquaintances, to be seen as an asset to Peyton instead of a liability. And everything had turned out so perfectly, despite Noreen Ellibee's presence, until—

"Stop brooding, sugar. What's done is done." Peyton placed his arm around her shoulder, drawing her close to his side. "A month from now, you'll be laughing about the whole thing."

"I doubt it." Tallie tried to scoot away from Peyton, but he held fast.

"What happened tonight wasn't your fault. It was Noreen's. Everyone at the party is well aware of what a witch she is."

"You know how it'll look in the paper tomorrow, don't you? It'll look like you socked Noreen in the mouth when she insulted me."

"And if the newspaper dares to even insinuate that that's what happened, I'll make a public statement explaining what actually happened and then sue the paper for libel."

"Yeah, and that'll be a great way to kick off your campaign for governor, won't it?"

Peyton kissed her on the forehead. "You worry too much, sugar."

"You certainly have changed your tune." Tallie wiggled, trying to escape from Peyton's hold. When he refused to release her, she turned in his arms, looking up at him. "For a man who's always been so concerned about his career, about his public image, about negative publicity, you sure don't seem worried that the name Peyton Rand is going to be mud when the morning papers hit the stands."

"I told you that you're overreacting, Tallie." Peyton lifted her onto his lap. When she didn't resist, he smiled. "Besides, my priorities are changing. I'm seeing my life and my career and my future in a whole new light."

Tallie slipped her arm around his neck. "Have you decided not to run for governor?"

"No, after tonight, I've definitely decided to run."

Squirming in his lap, Tallie became aware of Peyton's blatant state of arousal. "Thinking about all that power turns you on?"

"Thinking about what I'd like to do to you turns me on." He kissed her throat, then traced the veins in her neck with his tongue.

"Were you and Noreen Ellibee lovers?"

"What?"

"Were you and Noreen—"

"I heard you!"

Tallie grabbed him by the chin, her fingers clutching the side of his jaw. "Well?"

"What the hell difference does it make? She has absolutely nothing to do with you and me or with our future." Peyton gazed into Tallie's eyes, hoping that she would understand that no other woman had ever mattered to him the way she did, least of all Noreen.

"You were lovers, weren't you? And she still wants you."

Peyton tossed Tallie onto the sofa, got up and walked across the room to stand in front of the empty fireplace. "All right, you want to know, I'll tell you. Noreen and I were lovers for a couple of months nearly ten years ago. I didn't love her. She didn't love me. Harold and Betty thought we'd make a perfect couple and they started talking marriage."

"And that's when you ended the relationship?"

"Tallie, you know there have been other women in my life. Not a lot, but several." Peyton rubbed his chin as he paced the floor. "None of my relationships have been serious."

"You considered asking Donna Fields to marry you," Tallie reminded him.

"Briefly. I knew that Donna would make a perfect political wife, and I like and admire her as a person. In all honesty, Tallie, there's something about Donna that reminds me of you."

"There is?"

"She's a loving, caring person, but I never could have married her and ruined both our lives. One thing I've learned about myself the last few months is that I am not going to become a carbon copy of my father. I'm not going to ruin other people's lives out of selfishness."

"If you married me, I'd make sure you walked the straight and narrow. Your life would never turn out like your father's if I were your wife." Suddenly, Tallie realized that she had just proposed to Peyton.

"Marriage, huh?" Marriage to Tallie would certainly keep his life from being dull, and she'd be sure to control any undesirable tendencies he'd inherited from Marshall Rand. And she would sleep in his bed every night.

"It might not look as bad when that photo of you socking Noreen shows up in the papers tomorrow if people thought you were defending your future wife's reputation."

"I think I could be persuaded to marry you." Peyton held out his open arms. "Why don't you come here and convince me."

Tallie didn't budge off the sofa. "I think you may be a little confused, Counselor. You're the one who's going to have to do the convincing. So far in this relationship, I'm the one who's made all the compromises. I'm the one who's been chasing you for years. I'm the one who's said I love you. I'm even the one who's done the proposing."

Peyton dropped his arms to his sides. "What are you getting at, Tallie?"

"If you marry me, look at what you're getting. I'm attractive, intelligent and good in bed. Right?"

"Right."

"I'm loyal, trustworthy and a real asset to you. Harold Glover thinks my enthusiasm for causes could be a plus for you, and Donna Fields pointed out that I can save you from your biggest fear—becoming just like your father. Am I correct?

"Yes, you're correct."

"I gave you my virginity." Tallie paused when she noticed Peyton glaring at her. "Well, I did! And I love you. I've never loved anyone else."

"I concede that you possess sterling qualities, that you're a rare and precious gem, that I probably don't deserve you." Peyton walked over to her, then knelt down in front of the sofa. "Is that what you wanted to hear, Tallie?"

"It'll do for starters." She couldn't make this easy on him; if she did, it would only hurt their relationship in the long run. She wanted all or nothing. Peyton was capable of so much more than he was offering. She knew the only way he would ever be able to escape his father's legacy and come to her a whole man was for her to force the issue.

He took her hands in his, bringing them to his lips for a kiss. "I'm practically down on my knees. Is that what you want, sugar? A proposal on bended knee?"

She smiled. He returned her smile. "That would be nice."

"All right." Peyton shifted around, kneeling before Tallie, still holding her hands. "Tallulah Bishop, will you do me the honor of becoming my wife?"

"What can you offer me, Peyt?"

Taken aback by her question, Peyton stared at her in disbelief. "What can I offer you?"

"Yes." Tallie pulled her hands out of his, stood up and looked down at Peyton. "I've told you what I can offer you. What can you offer me? You can't offer me your virginity, but I'm willing to overlook that fault if—"

Rising to his feet in one swift motion, Peyton grabbed her by the shoulders. "You're willing to overlook that fault if what?"

"If you tell me that you love me, that you've never loved anyone else the way you love me." She bit back the tears stinging her eyes, burning her throat.

"You want me to tell you that..." He had never told anyone that he loved them. Love had not been a word in his father's or grandmother's vocabularies. Duty. Social position. Success. Money. Those were Rand words. Words by which to plan your future. Words to live by. But love? How could he tell Tallie that he loved her when he wasn't sure he even knew what love was?

"Is the question so difficult?" she asked, knowing full well that Peyt would have to fight the demons within him and win the battle before he could profess his love.

"Tallie, you know how I feel about you. Just being near you drives me crazy. All I can think about is you, being with you, kissing you, making love to you. I've asked you to marry me. Isn't that enough?" He tightened his hold on her shoulders.

"No, Peyt, it isn't enough." Jerking away from him, she walked toward the bedroom, pausing briefly in the open doorway. "I'm going to change back into my dress. Then I want you to drive me home."

"I don't want you to leave. I want you to stay. I want us to be together."

"But I don't want to stay," she lied. More than anything, she wanted to run to him, throw her arms around him and tell him that he didn't have to tear his soul apart to find the courage to love her. But for his sake as much as her own, she would not make it easy for him.

"You want me to say that I love you?" He stomped across the room, stopping only a few inches from her. "I'm a lawyer. Words are part of my business. I can talk my way out of any situation. If you want to hear the damned words, then I can say them."

"And when you say them, will you mean them?"

"Dammit, Tallie, why are you doing this?"

"Take me home, Peyt. Then you can think about me and yourself and your past and our future. I'm not going anywhere. I'll be in Crooked Oak waiting for you when you figure out that you love me." Tallie went into his bedroom, discarded his robe and slipped into her slightly damp black dress.

Ten

_____

The first thing she'd done when she awoke after a fitful night of restless sleep was rush outside for the newspaper, expecting to see the photograph of Peyton slugging Noreen Ellibee on the front page. There was no photograph, and the only mention of Peyton Rand and Tallulah Bishop had been in connection with their attendance at the Glovers' party, and that the two were now a "couple."

Tallie had been tempted to call Peyt and ask him how he'd kept the picture or any mention of the incident out of the paper. She wouldn't, she couldn't do that, she'd told herself. Sooner or later, he would contact her, and she could ask him if her suspicions were correct. Undoubtedly, Harold Glover possessed the power to control the media, enough to protect not only his stepdaughter but his good friend and the future governor.

Peyton hadn't contacted Tallie until eleven that morning when she had received a card along with an enormous bouquet of lilies and roses. The card read, "I want to see you tonight."

She had called him immediately, but had gotten his answering machine. She'd left a message, telling him that she would be waiting.

The rest of the day had gone by in a blur of activity for Tallie. She'd cleaned her house from top to bottom, straightening, dusting, mopping, vacuuming, rearranging. She'd shopped for steaks and a bottle of expensive wine. And she'd splurged on another new dress. A pink cotton sundress with an indecently low-cut neckline. No matter what happened tonight, she wanted everything to be perfect. Even knowing that Peyton might tell her that he didn't love her, she wanted to be prepared for the alternative—for the words she had waited most of her life to hear. She would not allow herself to dwell on the possibility that she had pushed Peyton too far with her ultimatum.

When she'd returned from her shopping trip, the message light on her answering machine blinked brightly. Peyton had called to tell her that he would arrive around seven-thirty.

She had taken Solomon into town with her, always aware of the necessity for his protection. When they'd returned home, she'd left him outside lying on the front porch, with Sheba asleep in the swing.

She checked the mantel clock in the living room. Seven o'clock, and she was ready. She'd taken a bubble bath, washed and dried her hair and splashed on the hundred-dollar-an-ounce perfume Caleb had sent her for her last birthday. The steaks were ready to grill, the potatoes baking in the oven and the salad greens prepared.

Music. Music and candlelight. Even though it was still daylight outside, the sun lay deep in the western horizon, slashes of summer orange and pink coloring the evening sky.

She put on her favorite Ricky Van Shelton tape, placed two tapering candles on the dining-room table and walked over to the open front door to gaze out at the winding road leading to her house. Soon. He'll be here soon, she told herself. And you'll know whether or not your gamble paid off.

"You're mighty dressed up, sexy gal."

Tallie froze to the spot when she heard the voice behind her, then turned quickly to come face-to-face with Eric Miller, a shiny .38 revolver in his hand.

"Surprised to see me?" He stood only a few feet away, his face flushed, his eyes bloodshot, a two-day growth of beard on his face. "Looks like you've got yourself all dolled up for pretty boy."

"How did you get in here?" Tallie backed up toward the front door, easing her hand behind her, trying to grab the handle. Solomon, who obviously heard Eric's voice, scratched at the door, growling.

"I picked the lock on your back door while you and that monster dog of yours went into town." Eric staggered toward her.

Tallie grabbed the storm-door handle, hoping to make it outside, away from Eric and to Solomon. Just as the door began to open, Eric reached around Tallie, slamming it shut and then locking it.

"Get that damned animal calmed down or I'll have to shoot him!" Sliding his arm around Tallie's waist, Eric shoved her up against his chest and laid the gun across her stomach.

"Quiet, Solomon," Tallie ordered. "Stay, boy. Stay."

Solomon sat upright, resting on his haunches. He continued whining for a few minutes, but when Tallie reiterated her order, he quieted, but stood watch just outside the closed glass door.

"Now, you and me are going to wait for your date." Eric slammed Tallie down on the sofa, then sat down beside her, clutching the gun in his hand.

"How do you know I have a date?" Tallie asked.

"You forget that I broke in while you was gone off buying yourself a new dress and fancy wine for pretty boy. I've been hiding in that big old closet over there." Eric pointed to the closet at the front end of the hallway. "I heard Rand's message when he called."

"Why did you break in, Eric? What...what do you want?"

He clutched Tallie's face in his big, sweaty hand, squeezing her cheeks. "What do I want? I want you, Tallie. Peyton Rand ain't the man for you, sexy gal. I am. I tried to get him out of your life before and I thought I'd done it, but no, you had to go get yourself all tied up with him again, didn't you?"

"What do you mean you tried to get him out of my life before?" Tallie's stomach quivered. Her hands dampened. She took several deep, calming breaths.

"I planned how I'd do it. It'd look like old Lobo or Cliff Nolan was out to get you." Eric slid his hand down Tallie's neck, circling her throat. "I stole some old codger's truck down in Mississippi, and as luck would have it, he had him a brand-new gun in the glove compartment."

"You...you shot Peyton?" Not Lobo Smothers. Not Cliff Nolan.

"I ain't much of a shot, but I thought I could wound him pretty bad or maybe even kill him if I got lucky." Eric drifted his hand downward until it rested just above Tallie's breasts, which swelled above the low-cut neckline of her sundress. "I didn't figure on how hard it would be to drive the truck and shoot at the same time."

"You were drunk, Eric. You didn't know what you were doing. Folks will understand."

"Ain't nobody going to know." Eric slipped his thumb down inside Tallie's dress, rubbing back and forth between her breasts.

She tried to move away, but Eric caught her, his meaty hand grabbing her by the back of the neck. "Once I get rid of Rand tonight, you and me are going on a little trip. A sort of honeymoon trip."

Tallie had no idea how she could escape from Eric, but she knew one thing for sure, she wasn't going to allow him to kill Peyton Rand. "We...we don't have to wait for Peyt."

"Sure we do. I don't want nobody standing between you and me." Eric ran his stubble-rough chin against Tallie's soft cheek.

"You and I...we could leave now. Go away. Just the two of us. We don't have to wait."

The distinct purr of the Jaguar's engine alerted both Eric and Tallie to Peyton's arrival. Solomon let out a low moan, never moving from his position on the porch.

Eric forced Tallie to her feet, twisting her arm behind her back. "We're going to go meet your lover boy." Eric held his gun in the hand he placed across Tallie's stomach.

Shoving her ahead of him, Eric positioned Tallie just to the side of the glass door, where Peyton wouldn't be able to see her from the front porch.

"When he knocks, tell him to come on in," Eric said.

Tallie looked down at the gun. Eric turned it away from her, aiming it toward the front door.

"Run, Peyt! Get out of here! He's going to shoot you!"

Throwing Tallie aside, Eric lunged at the door, barreling outside onto the porch.

Tallie picked herself up off the floor, flung open the storm door and rushed out directly behind Eric.

When he'd heard Tallie's screams, Peyton had managed to step to one side before Eric came crashing through the door. With only seconds to act, he lifted his foot high enough to trip Miller, who fell facedown onto the porch. The force of the fall knocked the breath out of Eric and loosened his hold on the revolver. Peyton kicked the gun out of Eric's hand. The weapon whizzed across the wooden floor and dropped off into the yard.

Winded but not unconscious, Eric hauled himself up, his big hands knotted into fists. "I'll kill you with my bare hands, pretty boy. It would have been quicker with a gun, but I just might enjoy this a whole lot more."

Peyton caught a glimpse of Tallie, wide-eyed and pale, standing beside Solomon. Eric lunged at Peyton, who landed a blow right into Eric's jaw. Reeling from the hit, Eric staggered, then swung at Peyton. Within minutes, the two men had exchanged several blows, Peyton knocking Eric into the yard. Although not as heavy as Eric, Peyton outmaneuvered him, finally landing a punch that knocked him to the ground.

Tallie ordered Solomon to attack, then rushed to retrieve the gun from where she'd seen it fall. Baring his sharp teeth, Solomon dashed past Peyton, plunging onto Eric, going directly for his throat.

Tallie held the gun in her trembling hands as she walked down the porch steps, Sheba following her. She called off Solomon, whose teeth had already broken the skin on Eric's neck. The Great Dane halted his attack, then stood guard over his prey.

"Eric's the one who shot you." Tears blurred Tallie's vision. "It was never Lobo or Cliff Nolan. Eric wanted you out of the way so he could have me."

"Here, sugar, you'd better let me have that." Peyton took the gun from Tallie. "You've saved the day, little heathen, now go call Lowell and let him take this big, dumb ape off our hands. I'll keep Mr. Miller company until the sheriff gets here."

* * *

With a cuffed Eric Miller in the back seat of Deputy Whitson's car, Lowell Redman instructed his officers to take their prisoner to jail.

Peyton held Tallie in his arms as they watched the car head down the driveway and toward the road. Feeling the tremors still racking Tallie's body, Peyton hugged her close, depositing tiny, comforting kisses on her forehead.

"I sure never thought Eric Miller was the man who shot you," Lowell said, lifting his hat off the porch swing. "Cliff Nolan's disappeared again. I guess he's off hunting Loretta. And Lobo will be standing trial pretty soon. He should get a little jail time. So it looks like we can stop worrying about Tallie's safety."

"I'll never stop worrying about Tallie's safety." Peyton touched her cheek with his fingertips. "But once she's the first lady of Tennessee, she'll be well protected at all times."

Jerking her head around, Tallie gazed up at Peyton, her mouth falling open when she saw the smile on his face.

"So that's the way it is, huh?" Lowell placed his hat on his head. "Doesn't surprise me a bit, and it won't come as a shock to folks in these parts. Everybody's known for years that you two were meant for each other."

"Well, it's come as a surprise to me," Tallie said. "Peyt hasn't even proposed to me yet."

"Well, I'd best be on my way so he can pop the question. Y'all can come down to the office in the morning. No need to bother coming by tonight." Lowell stepped down off the porch. "If you do run for governor, Peyt, you know you've already got everybody's vote in this part of the state. And once the rest of the state meets Crooked Oak's Tallie Bishop, you'll get their vote, too."

Not waiting to see Lowell off, Peyton lifted Tallie in his arms, eager to find a moment's privacy with her. Sheba jumped up on the porch swing, curling herself into a contented ball. Solomon spread out directly in front of the door.

"Peyt?"

Once inside, he carried her to the sofa, set her down and then on bended knee took her left hand in his. "Tallulah Bishop. I want you to be my wife." Grappling inside the pocket of his dusty, torn coat, Peyton brought out a jeweler's box and snapped open the lid. A dazzling four-carat diamond winked at Tallie from its velvet bed.

"Couldn't you find me a bigger one?" Touching the sparkling gem, Tallie laughed.

"Is it too big, sugar?" Removing the ring from the box, Peyton held it in front of her. "I almost bought something really big, but I thought about how tiny your fingers are."

"It's beautiful, Peyt." She held out her hand for him to place the ring on her finger. "I want to marry you. I want to be your wife, but I need to know...you have to tell me—"

"I love you, Tallie." He eased the diamond onto her finger, then lifted her hand to his lips. "I've never loved anyone the way I love you."

"Oh, Peyt. I had such a perfect evening planned. Steaks and good wine and me." She clutched the neckline of her sundress.

"You were pretty sure of me, weren't you, sugar?" Peyton grinned, a sense of sublime joy overwhelming him. He couldn't understand why it had taken him so long to admit his feelings, to accept the fact that no other woman on earth would have suited him half as well as Tallie. In his heart, he knew that she was his salvation. With her pure, compassionate, crusading soul as a guide for his Rand breeding, he no longer feared that he would repeat his father's mistakes.

"I wasn't sure of you, Peyt." Tallie took his face in her hands, pulling him close. "I only knew how much I loved you, and I was counting on your being smart enough to realize that I'm the best thing that could have happened to you." She kissed him. Quick and hard. "Even Harold Glover agrees with Donna that I'm an asset to you and not a liability."

Peyton lifted Tallie onto his lap, gripping the back of her head with his hand. "I've come to realize something that you should know, Tallie. You're far more important to me than anything else in this world, and that includes a political career. I'd still want to marry you and spend the rest of my life with you, even if it meant I'd never have a chance at becoming governor."

"You love me that much?" Tears trickled down Tallie's cheeks.

"I love you that much." He kissed her teardrops. "I just don't know why it's taken me so long to come to my senses."

"Because you've always been scared of me." Tallie began unbuttoning his shirt. "You've wanted me for just about as long as I've wanted you, but you were afraid to admit it."

Leaning forward on the sofa, Peyton discarded his soiled jacket, then lay back against the cushions, resting his head on the sofa arm while Tallie snuggled between his legs and continued undressing him.

"I used to catch myself fantasizing about you in the middle of the day when I was trying to work," he told her, raising his shoulders up where she could remove his shirt. "I'd get so horny, I'd turn into a raving madman and make life hell for everyone around me the rest of the day."

"What was I doing in your fantasies?" Tallie undid his belt.

Peyton grinned. "You were forcing me to have sex with you. I'd protest, state all the reasons why we shouldn't make love, but you wouldn't stop. You'd undress me and have your way with me."

"Mmm-hmm." Tallie glanced down at the huge diamond on her finger, the evening light from the windows touching it with a hazy pink glow, creating muted sparkles. "Since you've fulfilled my most cherished fantasy by telling me you love me and asking me to be your wife, I think I should fulfill your fantasy."

"I think that's fair," Peyton said.

"You, Mr. Rand, have absolutely no say-so in this. I'm going to strip you naked." She jerked down the zipper of his pants. "Then I'm going to kiss and lick and taste every inch of that big, hard body of yours. I'm going to drive you wild and when you think you can't take any more, I'm going to . . ." Lying down atop his body, her breasts pressing into his chest, she whispered in his ear precisely what she intended to do to him.

"Tallie Bishop, a lady shouldn't know such language." Peyton slid his hands up underneath her dress, caressing the backs of her legs as he eased upward to clutch her buttocks.

"I'm no lady, Peyt. You should know that. I'm a woman who grew up with three very outspoken big brothers who usually forgot to watch what they said around me." Tallie licked his throat. Circling first one nipple with the tip of her tongue, she ran her hand down inside his open slacks as she paid equal attention to its mate.

"For someone who was a virgin a week ago, you sure have learned fast." Peyton pushed her down against his arousal.

"You make me want to learn everything there is to know about lovemaking." Tallie grabbed his pants, tugging on them until he raised his hips so she could slip them down and over his legs.

"What other words and phrases did you overhear your big brothers saying?" Peyton kicked his slacks onto the floor.

Tallie blushed. "You like it when I tell you what I want to do to you?"

"I like it when you look at me, touch me, kiss me and when you make love with me." Peyton grabbed her, pulling her to him, taking her mouth with complete loving passion.

When the kiss ended, Tallie lay on top of him, her breathing ragged as she listened to his wildly beating heart. "I love you so much, Peyt. Sometimes I love you so much, it hurts."

"I know what you mean, sugar. I never knew I could love anybody, want anybody, *need* anybody the way I do you." Lifting her skirt, he hooked his fingers inside the elastic of her bikini panties and eased them downward. "I know it's crazy, but . . . I need you, Tallie. I need you like I need air to breathe."

Her dress flew off over her head, landing in a pink cloud on the wooden floor, her strapless bra following. Then Peyton's briefs joined the heap.

Tallie kept her promise, learning every hard, masculine inch of Peyton's body, stopping to savor the most delicious parts, driving him to the brink of madness as her untutored mouth learned one of the age-old, courtesans' techniques for pleasuring a man.

By the time Tallie drew the last drops of control from Peyton's body, he toppled her over onto the floor, both of them frenzied with an elemental hunger that bordered on insanity.

"You're wild with wanting it, aren't you, little heathen?" Peyton lifted her hips in his hands, spreading her legs as he prepared a place for himself. "You're hurting as much as I am."

"I'm dying, Peyt, dying. Take me. Please. Now!" She grabbed his shoulders when he rammed into her, bending her knees, clutching him around the waist with her legs, lifting herself to meet each powerful lunge.

In a tumult of overwhelming, uncontrolled lust, man took woman and woman took man. They mated in nature's procreative dance, coupling with the same red-hot drive with which lovers have exchanged pleasures since time immemorial. Tallie and Peyton made love, the rich fullness of their animal natures enhanced by the beauty of the true love in their hearts and the timeless passion in their souls.

In the moment of completion, their bodies slick with sweat, they cried out their fulfillment as ecstasy claimed them.

Peyton leaned over and kissed Tallie, then lifted her to her feet. "Right now, I can barely walk," he told her. "But I know this wasn't enough. I'll never get enough of you."

"Let's go to bed." Tallie slipped her arm around his waist. "I have satin sheets on my bed."

"You hussy."

"When it comes to you, Peyton Rand, I am a hussy."

"Don't ever change, sugar. I like everything about you just the way it is."

When they fell into the bed, Tallie snuggled against Peyton, her hand resting on his chest, her fingers twisting into his hair. "Oh, we'll both change, and the changes will be good for us. But there's one thing that will never change."

"What's that?" He cupped her naked hip in his hand.

"I'm always going to give you a hard time."

Peyton burst into laughter, dragging Tallie off the bed and over on top of him. "Is that a promise?"

Gliding her hand downward, circling him with her strong little hand, Tallie whispered what she intended doing to him, then laid her head against his heart and vowed loudly, "That is a promise."

Epilogue

Six months pregnant, a radiantly beautiful Tallulah Rand held the bible on which her husband laid his hand while being sworn in as the new governor of Tennessee. It was a precious moment that would live in Tallie's heart forever. Together, she and Peyton had planned and worked and achieved their dream.

Never had two such mismatched lovers been so perfect for each other. Even though each of them had retained the essence of their personalities after they married, they had each changed in subtle ways as they learned to compromise. Peyton had helped Tallie learn to think before acting, and she had taught him to trust his own emotions.

When the swearing-in ceremony ended, Peyton drew Tallie into his arms, kissing her boldly, there before God, Spence and his family, their friends, their acquaintances and, via television, the entire state of Tennessee.

"Welcome to Nashville, Mrs. Rand," Peyton said, nuzzling her ear. "Did you ever think we'd make it?"

"I never doubted for a moment that you would become governor. This was your destiny."

"It would have all been meaningless without you, sugar." Peyton led Tallie down the steps and through the crowd of well-wishers and reporters.

"Yeah, well, I'm just glad my big brother had the good sense to marry you, Tallie," Spence said as he put his arm around Pattie, and their family followed Peyton and Tallie toward the waiting limousine. "Now I don't have to worry about him turning into just another crooked politician."

Speaking loud enough for only those closest to him to hear, Peyton said, "That's not something I have to worry about as long as Tallie's at my side. This little heathen has kept me on my toes since the day I met her, and she's still nothing but trouble for me. You wouldn't believe all the things she expects me to accomplish in my first four years as governor."

"I have no doubt that you'll accomplish everything she's expecting of you," Spence said.

"I'm sure going to try. I never want to let Tallie down, not as long as I live."

Together, Peyton and Tallie turned to face the reporters, smiling and waving and speaking to the ones they recognized, calling them by name.

The evening papers would show two pictures side by side on the front page. One of an adoring Tallulah Rand watching her husband being sworn in as governor. The other of the new governor and his first lady waving at the crowd, one of the governor's arms draped lovingly around his wife's shoulders, his other arm crossing her waist, his hand resting possessively on her round stomach.

* * * * *

JINGLE BELLS, WEDDING BELLS:
Silhouette's Christmas Collection for 1994

Christmas Wish List

*To beat the crowds at the malls and get the perfect present for *everyone,* even that snoopy Mrs. Smith next door!

*To get through the holiday parties without running my panty hose.

*To bake cookies, decorate the house and serve the perfect Christmas dinner—just like the women in all those magazines.

*To sit down, curl up and read my Silhouette Christmas stories!

Join *New York Times* bestselling author Nora Roberts, along with popular writers Barbara Boswell, Myrna Temte and Elizabeth August, as we celebrate the joys of Christmas—and the magic of marriage—with

JINGLE BELLS, WEDDING BELLS

Silhouette's Christmas Collection for 1994.

MIRA™

The brightest star in women's fiction!

This October, reach for the stars and watch all your dreams come true with **MIRA BOOKS.**

HEATHER GRAHAM POZZESSERE
Slow Burn in October
An enthralling tale of murder and passion set against the dark and glittering world of Miami.

SANDRA BROWN
The Devil's Own in November
She made a deal with the devil...but she didn't bargain on losing her heart.

BARBARA BRETTON
Tomorrow & Always in November
Unlikely lovers from very different worlds... They had to cross time to find one another.

PENNY JORDAN
For Better For Worse in December
Three couples, three dreams—can they rekindle the love and passion that first brought them together?

The sky has no limit with **MIRA BOOKS.**

SILHOUETTE®

Desire®

Big Bad
WOLFE

WOLFE WANTING
by Joan Hohl

Don't miss *Wolfe Wanting,* Book 3 of Joan Hohl's
seductively sexy BIG BAD WOLFE series, coming your
way in October...only from Silhouette Desire.

As sergeant for the Pennsylvania State Police
Department, Royce Wolfe was just doing his job—
protecting a violent-crime victim, making sure she
was safe. But he deserved a slap in the face for what
he was thinking about the sexy woman. He wanted
her—bad. But a Big *Bad* Wolfe was the last thing
Megan Delaney needed....

SDJH3

SILHOUETTE... Where Passion Lives

Don't miss these Silhouette favorites by some of our most distinguished authors! And now you can receive a discount by ordering two or more titles!

SD#05750	BLUE SKY GUY by Carole Buck	$2.89 ☐
SD#05820	KEEGAN'S HUNT by Dixie Browning	$2.99 ☐
SD#05833	PRIVATE REASONS by Justine Davis	$2.99 ☐
IM#07536	BEYOND ALL REASON by Judith Duncan	$3.50 ☐
IM#07544	MIDNIGHT MAN by Barbara Faith	$3.50 ☐
IM#07547	A WANTED MAN by Kathleen Creighton	$3.50 ☐
SSE#09761	THE OLDER MAN by Laurey Bright	$3.39 ☐
SSE#09809	MAN OF THE FAMILY by Andrea Edwards	$3.39 ☐
SSE#09867	WHEN STARS COLLIDE by Patricia Coughlin	$3.50 ☐
SR#08849	EVERY NIGHT AT EIGHT by Marion Smith Collins	$2.59 ☐
SR#08897	WAKE UP LITTLE SUSIE by Pepper Adams	$2.69 ☐
SR#08941	SOMETHING OLD by Toni Collins	$2.75 ☐

(limited quantities available on certain titles)

TOTAL AMOUNT	$_____
DEDUCT: 10% DISCOUNT FOR 2+ BOOKS	$_____
POSTAGE & HANDLING	$_____
($1.00 for one book, 50¢ for each additional)	
APPLICABLE TAXES*	$_____
TOTAL PAYABLE	$_____
(check or money order—please do not send cash)	

To order, complete this form and send it, along with a check or money order for the total above, payable to Silhouette Books, to: **In the U.S.:** 3010 Walden Avenue, P.O. Box 9077, Buffalo, NY 14269-9077; **In Canada:** P.O. Box 636, Fort Erie, Ontario, L2A 5X3.

Name:_____

Address:_____ City:_____

State/Prov.:_____ Zip/Postal Code:_____

*New York residents remit applicable sales taxes.
Canadian residents remit applicable GST and provincial taxes.

SBACK-SN

Silhouette®
™